DANIEL WEISBECK

MOON RISING

BOOK ONE OF

THE UPSILON SERIES

Publisher, Copyright, and Additional Information

Moon Rising by Daniel Weisbeck, published by DJW Books

www.danielweisbeckbooks.com

Cover design by Théa Magerand

Edited by Lauren Humphries-Brooks

PART 01_

_JENNA

ONE

I CAN HEAR his heavy footsteps even when he isn't here. That horrifying sound of feet plodding and wood creaking above me. The thought of it is enough to make me run and hide in my corner. There is a slight drag from one of his feet when he walks. I like to imagine that foot is resisting him, fighting his advance. That foot knows better.

My room is dark but not the kind of dark you see when you close your eyes. Twenty-nine strips of light, faint and narrow, bleed through the cracks of the wooden planks over my head and line the cold cement floor in my room. It's just enough light for me to see everything within these four walls. Although there isn't much to see, to be honest. I have a discoloured metal cot with a thin mattress, no pillow or sheets, and a small night-stand alongside it. On the nightstand is a child's lamp. The ceramic base is in the shape of a pink elephant with its trunk lifted high over its head,

1

disappearing under the lavender shade where the tip of its nose holds the usually unlit light bulb. The lavender shade is covered in four different images of cartoon elephants that repeat across the surface. Whoever made this lamp wanted the elephant images to seem random, but I can easily see the pattern.

Every fourth elephant is wearing an old-fashioned hat shaped like an upside-down bowl. He looks directly at me while holding an open umbrella over his head. I still don't understand why he needs both an umbrella and a hat.

Every third image is a plump elephant dressed in a pink ballerina skirt. She stands on the toe-tips of her right foot while her other foot rests on the inside of her opposite calf. She is graceful, but I get the feeling she is tired of holding the same position.

The next figure is a large mother elephant facing sideways as her infant follows close behind her. His thick trunk is twisted around her thin tail. They will be together forever.

The last image is a lone baby elephant. He (it looks like a boy to me) sits on his bottom with his right hand over his head, holding a string attached to a red balloon. This baby elephant has a wicked smile. However, something is not right with him. Maybe he has been left behind because he is naughty, or perhaps he ran away. Either way, I don't spend too much time looking at him. I prefer the elephant in the pink ballerina skirt.

On the opposite side of the room from my

bed, near the foot of the wooden staircase, is a metal folding chair with a grey plastic seat. I don't sit on this chair because that is where he sits when he comes to visit. When he isn't down here, staring at me, I mostly sit on the floor. Mainly in the corner opposite both the mattress and chair. This is the farthest and darkest part of my room, where nobody can see me. Here I am safe.

To pass the time between his visits, I count in my head. I've been locked away in this room precisely thirty-one days almost to the hour. I know this because I have an innate sense of timing. Or that's what my teacher tells me.

"Child, you must have an atomic clock in your brain. You always know exactly what time it is," my teacher would say and then let out a small laugh.

I smile when she says this. I like it when Teacher notices me. Or noticed me. The thought of not seeing my teacher again makes me sad. I wonder if she even thinks about me anymore. Someone must have told her I was missing. She would worry, but she has a lot of children to worry about. I wasn't unique except for my ability to know the time so well. So maybe she has already forgotten about me.

The only other piece of furniture in my room is a three-drawer dresser. It's painted white and has gold and glass knobs for handles. The drawers are full of girls' clothing meant to be worn by a ten- or eleven-year-old. The top drawer is full of white underpants. The second drawer is filled with tops. And the bottom drawer is stacked with three kinds of bottoms: trousers, skirts, and summer shorts. I can barely fit into these clothes. But he insists I wear them. I have no choice anyway, as he took my clothes away. He even picks out which ones he wants to see me in at the end of each visit for the next time. As soon as he leaves, I put on the only nightgown I have down here. It's long and light blue with tiny white daisies all over it. This fits me better than most of the other stuff. I guess it's pretty, but I can't help myself from hating it. I hate all these clothes. I think someone else used to wear them. They aren't entirely worn, but neither are they brand new. I feel like they belonged to someone he knew or someone he wants me to be. I still haven't quite figured that part out yet.

I think my room is somewhere below his house. I capture glimpses of the area above me when he opens the trapdoor. Slivers of grey cement walls and artificial fluorescent lights make me think I'm in a hole dug into his basement floor. Above me, I can see a wall filled with tools hanging on a pegboard: saws, hammers, an axe, stuff like that. Stuff a dad would have in his basement to fix things around the house. That's why I think I'm in his basement. That's all I know about where I am.

Every day he comes down at six in the evening. He turns on the elephant light, first from outside, giving it power, and then inside the room by twisting the little knob sticking out of the elephant's mouth like a tongue. Then he takes a seat in his chair, facing me. He never says a word. There is a deep sadness in his wet eyes. But I don't care. I want to kill him. I want to run over and start hitting him until he is unconscious so I can get out of here. But I don't. And I never say anything. I keep quiet. I learned that early on. Boy, did I. When I ask questions, he stops visiting. So now I don't say a word. I need the light on for a bit of time, at least.

I forgot there is one other thing down here, a book about a giving tree. Its cover is slightly stained, and the pages are warped like it was damaged in water and fire. Sometimes I flip through the book while he is staring at me. I don't need to read it anymore. I know the story by heart. I just look at the pictures and let my brain tell me the story. This helps pass the time during his visits.

It's almost six. I can feel it. He will be here soon. I must get dressed now.

TWO

THIS TOP IS TOO SHORT. And it's itchy. Today he wants me to wear blue shorts with frilly white lace around the legs. Why did he pick these clothes? This top and these shorts together? They don't really go. A thick wool top with shorts—who would wear these at the same time? It's like a child who didn't know any better picked these, not a full-grown man. I'm starting to wonder if Sad-man (that's what I call him) is a little slow.

He's coming. I can hear that drag and shuffle. It's slight. Soon he will turn on the power to my room. I can almost count the steps until I hear the *click* of the switch. There! That was it. Now he will lift the lid on my room and *clop, clop, clop* down the wooden steps. But not before he turns around and locks us inside. The *clinking* of chains and keys and padlock is familiar to me now. These sounds are like a doorbell or the *ring-a-la-ding* of a phone. They always announce someone is coming —or arrived.

I'm sitting on the side of my bed wearing these stupid clothes he left out when he approaches me. Leaning over, he turns on the elephant light. His smell is familiar. Always the same oily jeans, like he has been working on a car or something mechanical. His shirt smells like soap and lilac. I think it's his laundry detergent. My clothes smell the same.

When he comes this close, I stare at his shoes because I don't want to see into his eyes. Every visit, he wears the same brown workman boots. The toes look hard. I can tell they are reinforced by how they have kept their shape. The rest of the boots are worn and cracked. I wouldn't want to be kicked by those boots. He could probably break my face with a hard end like that.

I think about that a lot. Ways he might hurt me. So far, he just sits quietly down here during his visits. But I can see his fists rolled so tight his knuckles are white. He pushes them deep into his thighs like he is kneading bread. Those fists are for me. I'm sure of it. If I speak or upset him, those boot tips or those fists are coming at me.

One time, during the first week, before I understood what he wanted from me, I refused to wear the clothes he left behind. I kept my night-gown on and sat in a ball in my dark corner of the room. When he saw me sitting there, rather than on the bed, he ran over and grabbed my arm so hard I wanted to scream, cry out, but all I could manage was a slight squeal. I was so scared I lost my voice for a second. He walked me over to the bed and threw me at it. My hip slammed against the metal frame, and I fell to my knees. He just stood there, hovering over me, waiting. I pulled myself up and sat on the bed, facing him. That seemed to calm him down. After that, he went and sat on his chair. I always wear the clothes he leaves out now.

His back is straight when he sits in the chair, as if he has a metal rod up his spine. He holds his knees together and points his feet forwards. He can sit like that for over an hour. I can't imagine what he is thinking about.

Today, he is watching me as usual. I'm picking at the fringe on my shorts, waiting until he leaves. The shorts are tight around my thighs when I sit down. I count the lace waves in my head: one, two, three, four, five... My finger trails the scratchy material.

"Pick up the book," he suddenly shouts.

This is new. Sad-man doesn't talk to me very much. There is a heavy thumping in my chest from my heart speeding up. I'm scared. All I can do is stare at him. His eyes are so green. I never noticed that before, or maybe I made myself forget. He has thick black hair that he wears shaved close to his head so that it looks like a shadow over his skull. His eyebrows are also thick black and shaped like two checkmarks facing each other. He is pale, almost sickly. The bottom half of his face is smooth like a little boy's, but deep wrinkles between his eyebrows and at the corners of his eyes make me think he is much older. He's wearing the same plaid shirt he always wears when visiting. I wonder if that's the only shirt he owns. Or maybe he has a closet full of the exact same shirt.

"Pick up the book!" he hollers at me again.

I quickly bend over and grab the tree book from the bottom shelf of the nightstand.

"Read it out loud."

I'm not sure my voice is going to work. I open the book. My mouth starts moving, but the sound is as low as a whisper and trembling.

"*The Giving Tree*. By Shel Silverstein."

I read the entire book. Sad-man says nothing. Doesn't even move. When I finish, I look at him from the corner of my eye. His face is wet, full of tears, but he isn't moving at all, and I can't hear him crying. I close the book and lay it on my lap with my hands over it and wait. We sit like that, in silence, for over twenty minutes. When he finally stands up, I jolt back, startled. Walking over to the dresser, he pulls out the bottom drawer. He takes out a new pair of pants for me: the yellow and burnt-orange plaid ones. I roll my eyes behind his back. Those pants are so ugly. I would never wear them if I was back outside. Then he takes out a puffy short-sleeved white blouse and lays them together on the top of the dresser, slowly, trying not to ruin the folding. After he is finished, he leaves.

The light is off again, and the ceiling is closed

and locked from the outside. I hear the scraping of furniture being pulled onto my ceiling and watch the tiny floating bits of dust fall through the light beam cracks. The object that sits on my roof casts a shadow on the ground—gaps in the light strips where the dark forms a solid circle. Once in a while, I sit in the shadow circle instead of my corner. I call this shadow my moon, and the light through the cracks my sunshine. Pretending helps me. When I sit under my moon, I often wonder about the outside. I don't mean the basement directly above me, but all the way outside where the real moon and sun live. I imagine a breeze blowing against my face, the tingling feeling of it moving through my long curly brown hair. I miss the wind. I miss the sounds of leaves twisting in the trees and birds singing. Teacher used to take us outside, and we would lay on our backs under the canopy of the small woodland behind our school. She would tell us to be quiet and listen. Then, after a few minutes, she would start to point out the different bird songs and tell us where they were coming from.

Robins were my favourite. You can tell a robin by their long and short trills mixed together into a beautiful song. It sounds like liquid silver pouring into the air, pure and crystal-like.

The great tit was always easy to identify. Hearing a tit always made us laugh because it sounds like it was calling for our teacher. "Tea-cher, Tea-cher," they would sing over and over. Sometimes she would answer the tit, our teacher, that is. She would look up into the trees with the shadows of leaves dancing on her face and say, "I'm here, great tit. I'm listening to your song. We're all listening."

I call wrens the soldiers of the woods. Their song starts with a loud marching chant and ends with a rapid gunfire salute at the end: "Tat, tat, tat, tat, tat."

The goldfinch's song reminds me of tuning an old-fashioned radio, all up and down sounds. And the song of a chiffchaff sounds just like its name: "Chiff-chaff, chiff-chaff, chiff-chaff." I really miss being outside.

When I go over to the dresser to pull out my nightgown and change out of these ridiculous shorts, I see something new. Next to the white blouse is a book. The cover is charred like it was in a fire. The entire upper left corner is missing as if it were burned off. The surface is padded in a pastel pink gingham material that is slightly grey from smoke. Glued on the fabric are the letters: A.F. on top and J. F. below. In between the top initials and bottom initials is a heart cut from red cloth. The book looks like it was made by a girl. I can't imagine Sad-man did this. It's pretty and kind of sweet looking. I pick it up, carry it over to the bed, and sit down. The elephant light is out now, so I must keep shifting the book between two light strips from overhead to see it clearly. On the first page is a handwritten message: *To my dearest Jenna. You are the stars in my sky, the sunshine in my day, and the seed that grows from my giving tree.*

The inside pages are thick cardboard with a shiny film clinging to the surface which can be peeled back. I turn to the next page, and there are six photos spread across the two facing pages. They are pressed underneath the plastic sheet— four on the left-hand page and two larger pictures on the right-hand page. The first images are of a young baby and someone I assume is its mother. They are holoprints. I've looked at holoprints like this in school when we studied different cultures from around the world.

I wave my hand over the first photo. A moving image of a naked baby shoots up into the air, hovering over the page. Its flesh is purple and covered in blood. The squirming newborn starts to cry. I'm assuming this is Jenna from the inscription on the first page. Even if it is not, I'll call her Jenna. And the mother in the pictures might be A. from the cover initials. I'll call her A. I feel I'm meant to look at these photos more than once, so it will be good to have a name for each of them. I wave my hand and turn off the squirming, screaming baby. I don't like the sound. In the next holoprint, A. holds a naked Jenna close to her exposed chest and plays with her tiny hands, kissing her forehead and smelling her skin. This holoprint is soundless. It might have been damaged by the fire that burned off the left corner. I can still make out some of the words A. is saying by watching her lips closely.

"I love you... My little seed... Come (then a word or name I can't make out) get in the picture." A. is waving at the person holding the recorder when she says this last bit, but whoever she is talking to remains unseen.

The following few pages are pictures of Jenna growing up. A baby in a bath. A child's first birthday party. Jenna learning to ride a bike. Stock photos of any childhood. Then I skip ahead to the last page with photos, but not the final page in the book, not by far, and it's Jenna much older, around ten or eleven. She is sitting on a swing tied to the branch of a large tree. The sun is behind her. She is smiling at the camera, swinging forwards with her feet high in the air. Her smile is sweet but also a little teasing. That's when I notice the shorts and top. She is wearing the wool pullover with the blue shorts laced on the legs that I am wearing. These are her clothes.

THREE

A SHADOW HAS FORMED in between the bars of light on the wall behind my bed. It keeps moving from the left to the right and then right to the left. I hear the scuffing foot. It is Sad-man walking back and forth above my door. He is early, but that's okay. I'm sitting on my bed, in the dark, and I have already put on the burnt-orange plaid trousers and white top he left out yesterday. When I pulled the white blouse over my head, I noticed a light-red stain on the front. The pale spot looks like it was washed many times to remove the smudge. I wonder what Jenna spilt on her shirt. Maybe she was eating a hotdog, and ketchup squirted out of the bun. No, it was cherry juice that spilt on her shirt while she was playing in the park. Or maybe it was blood. Jenna was a bit of a tomboy. There is a picture of her climbing a large old tree in the album. She is very high up, and the person taking the holoprint recording is standing on the ground, pointing the camera at her. Jenna is straddling a large branch with her legs hanging on either side like she's riding a horse. There is no fear in her smile as she lifts both hands off the tree at the same time and waves them high in the air. I'm frightened for her. This is a girl who got hurt and didn't care. Jenna had scrapes and scars from playing hard. Yes, this is the correct answer. The stain is blood. She got cut while playing outside. Maybe running too fast near a broken fence. Her mother came out when she started crying and helped her. A. cleaned Jenna up and placed a Band-aid on her cut, gave her a little kiss on the forehead, and then set about washing Jenna's favourite shirt over and over again, trying to get the stain out.

Jenna is lucky to have such a loving mother.

Sad-man is still pacing back and forth up there. He is late for his six o'clock visit by precisely five minutes. I wonder why he isn't down here yet. The elephant light is still off. I tried twisting its tongue a few times, but he hasn't turned the power on yet. The album is back where he left it after his last visit. I spent the night replaying all the holoprints and thinking about Jenna and A.'s life together. In some strange way, having them in my mind makes me feel less afraid. Like I'm not alone in my room anymore. I feel stronger today. I have a new imaginary place where I can go when Sad-man stares at me. I'm there now. Watching Jenna play outside is like a dream. Sometimes I'm her friend, playing along, and other times I am Jenna. I can see the world through her eyes. Of course, I still have my own feelings, even when I'm Jenna. But I ride her body like a kite in the sky, soaring away and pulling hard on the string that holds me to my room.

The trapdoor over the staircase is opening. Sad-man clomps down the steps slowly. He is wearing blue jeans and his work boots again, but I notice he is wearing a new shirt when I can see above his waistline. It is a sporting top: dark red with a big number eighteen on the front and the word "VIKINGS" embossed over the number. The shirt is crumpled like it's been on the floor in a pile for a long time. He locks the door overhead behind him, walks silently over to my bed, and bending over, he turns on the elephant light. Stuffy mildew and maybe sweat—that's what the shirt smells like.

Sad-man heads over to the dresser before sitting in the chair today. All these new behaviours are scaring me. My knuckles are tight as I squeeze the mattress edge for support. I know nothing can really help me now but holding onto something stops my hands from thrashing like a crazy person. I can feel screams sitting in my belly, scratching at my throat, trying to escape. I have to keep them in. An image of Jenna pops into my head. I'm inside Jenna, looking down from the tree branch. Sad-man is on the ground holding the camera pointed at me while I laugh and smile for him. This Sad-man won't hurt me. I can feel my grip loosen as the shrieking in my mind fades. Not gone, mind you, but turned down like the volume on a media player.

He puts a hand on the album cover lying on the dresser top, where he left it. I've purposely put it back exactly as I found it. I don't want him to know I've been looking at it. Wait, that's not right. I don't care if he knows I've been looking at it. But I want him to wonder. I want him to not know what has happened down here in my room and what might happen. Let him be the one confused and guessing for once; I laugh in my head. A sudden urge to jump up and attack Sad-man rages through my body. But one glance at the chains and locks on the door, and his hard-toed boots, reminds me to sit quietly.

He is tracing the initials on the book with his fingertips. The movement is gentle. The album, these holoprints, Jenna and A., were important to Sad-man. But there is something wrong—something cruel in the way his shoulders slump forwards and his head hangs low, yet his back is stiff and rigid, and his left fist is squeezed tight. I have a horrible feeling. I'm scared for Jenna and A. I can imagine Sad-man hunting them. Maybe he snuck into A.'s house at night and stole this album. He is capable of that. However, this doesn't feel right.

Maybe Jenna and A. are his family. Yes, that feels correct. They are his family, and I am wearing Jenna's clothes. But that is too easy, too kind. He must have done something to them. Sad-man killed Jenna and A.—his family. I can believe that. Sad-man can kill. The veins that appear on both sides of his temples and the way his eyes narrow and squint hard when he gets ready to leave tells the truth about Sad-man. He is angry and wants something. A shiver runs down my spine as I finally understand. Sad-man wants me to be Jenna.

Sad-man opens the album. I can hear plastic peeling back as he removes a holoprint. Then, turning, he brings one of the printed images over to me and holds it up to my face. It is the picture of A. holding a newborn Jenna against her bare chest.

"What's her name?" he says with hard, slow words.

I just look up at the picture. Suddenly I have doubts. I don't know anything. They no longer look like A. and Jenna. They are strangers. People I don't know.

He shoves the holoprint a little closer to my face, the tips of his fingers colourless as he pinches the edge tight. "Who is this!" he screams while shaking the photo at me.

I want to cry. I can feel pools of water on my bottom eyelids. "A.," I say in a quiet voice. Even I can hardly hear myself.

Sad-man's face pinches and twists in confusion and rage. I'm wrong. I quickly raise both my arms to block my face. I'm glad I did because his left fist is coming for my head. I brace myself and let out a little squeal. I close my eyes tight, sending my tears racing down my cheeks. "Please," I whisper to him—to anyone.

Nothing hits me. I can hear his heavy breathing. I open one eye. His fist is there, hovering right in front of my face, frozen.

"You stupid girl." He spits when speaking.

For a few minutes, Sad-man just stares at me. I've dropped my arms, but I'm still turned away. I can't look at his eyes anymore. They are desperate, and I know I'm going to disappoint him again. Through the corner of my eye, I watch him walk back to the dresser. As calm as a bird on a spring morning, as if nothing had just happened, he places the photo back in the album, closes the book, and pulls out my outfit for tomorrow. He turns to leave. When the trapdoor locks and the elephant light blinks off, I finally relax my shoulders.

I can't move for about an hour. I try everything to forget what just happened. I think of Jenna and A. laughing together. I think of the birds in the woods behind the school. I think of my moon. But none of it is working. I hate Sad-man. No, that's not right. Sad-man hates me. I've failed him in some way. If I could only make him happy, make him believe I was Jenna, he might be nicer to me. Maybe, just maybe, if I can get him to believe he loves me, I can get out of here. Yes, this makes sense. I now have a plan.

FOUR

THE MOON IS a little more to the right tonight. It's positioned over the trapdoor so that the left side is directly on one of the boards, giving it a flat edge like it has been cut off. I'm thinking of all the different forms my moon has had since I've been down here: a complete circle, an arc. Once, it had straight edges on opposite sides so that it looked like someone was squeezing it. There are many variations I have seen. Thirty-two, to be exact, the same number of nights I've been here.

I didn't sleep last night. I was thinking of ways to get Sad-man to love me. I started to put Jenna together. I thought of all the clues—the book of the giving tree, Jenna's album of holoprints, her clothes—until I had a complete person in my mind. Once I had a whole idea of who Jenna was and what she liked, I started the next phase of my plan, to create memories of my life as Jenna. I paced around my moon in bare feet. My nightgown floated through the light beams like a firefly flying through a forest at night: on and off, my body blinked. Hours passed, and I managed to create at least one hundred scenarios in my mind of moments that made Jenna happy: her favourite birthday party, a sleepover she had with her best friend (because Jenna would have loads of friends), watching a funny movie with Sad-man and A.; on and on I went, one story after another. So great were the details that I really began to feel my own memories blending with Jenna's until everything sat in my head like one bowl of mushy soup.

At five, I prepare to get dressed for Sad-man's visit. This is much earlier than I usually prepare for his visit. But today is special. And something of the lavender-coloured dress he had laid out had caught my attention in a way none of Jenna's clothes had before. I found my eye wandering to the dresser several times throughout the day. It is a summer dress, with shoulder straps rather than sleeves. A box-cut top section comes down to the waist, where a horizontal seam connects it to a slightly wider skirt of the same material. The dress is simple. So simple it could have been anybody's dress. Yet I felt...it was mine, and I felt happy, yes, delighted at seeing it. I wore this dress on a trip to the ocean with A. and Sad-man. It hung loosely around my body and swayed easily when I ran on the beach. The sun was hot that day, and the dress let just enough breeze through to keep me cool and was long enough to shade me from the hot sun. I especially liked how I could lift the skirt when I sat down to feel the warm sand along the back of my legs. It felt private, like being naked and not naked at the same time.

The beach trip that day wasn't planned, so we hadn't packed anything, not even swimming suits. Sad-man wanted to surprise A. and me. Well, he mostly wanted to surprise A., who loved the ocean. This day was a celebration for them. An anniversary of the day they met. I remember the seagulls singing as they circled over our heads. "More, more, more, more..." the white arrow birds screamed, begging us for some of the lunch Sad-man had secretly put together in a lovely wicker hamper. With my feet buried under the warm gold beads of the beach, we ate peanut butter and jelly sandwiches and tried to keep the sand from getting into the peanut butter. Sad-man wasn't a good cook. A. laughed when she saw what he had made, but she also loved it. I could tell by the way she smiled and looked at him with warm moist eyes as he unwrapped the sandwiches like they were a delicacy. A. truly loved Sad-man. He wasn't perfect, but she found a way to look past his faults. And Sad-man knew he wasn't perfect, which only made him love A. even more for loving him. Anyway, this is the memory I now have of the lavender dress.

I pick up the dress from the dresser top. An instant feeling of warm sun and silky-smooth sand under my feet washes through me. I take off my nightgown and slip the dress over my head. Like all of Jenna's clothes, the dress is a little too small for me. It should just fall onto my shoulders loosely, but it gets stuck around my chest, and I have to tug it down to help it fit. I must have grown since the last time I wore it. How long ago was that? We visited the beach when I was eleven, so a year ago. That's right, it had been a year since we visited the beach as a happy family.

A noise from above distracts me from my happy memories—the sound of footsteps and a slight drag. Sad-man is coming. My breath is short. I feel excited and nervous rather than scared. I'm going to share my memories with Sad-man. It is a dangerous plan. I know that. If he doesn't think I am Jenna, he might hurt me. So, I have to be careful and go slow.

Click, I hear power turning on in my room from outside. Then the clanking of keys and locks from above. I can hardly think, I'm so nervous. Jenna, summer, beach, A.'s smile, Sad-man's sandwiches, I keep them tight in my mind, rehearsed, afraid I might get it wrong.

I'm sitting on my bed in the lavender dress he left out when I see him come down the stairs.

He doesn't seem angry. Typical, that's how I would describe him today. His face is straight, and his eyes look lost, far away. I want him to look at me to see the dress I'm wearing. If he does, he doesn't show any reaction. Leaning in, he twists the elephant's tongue. The *click, click, click* of the dial mirrors the rapid beating in my chest.

"Thank you." The words just pop out of my

mouth. I instantly feel like it was too fast, too obvious.

Sad-man spins around and looks at me with narrow eyes. I want to crawl up into the corner of my bed against the wall. He tilts his head and pinches his eyebrows together.

"Okay. Thank you for what?" he says.

"Thank you for the dress. I love this dress. The colour is so pretty. Thank you for the peanut butter and jelly sandwich on the beach. I really like your sandwiches and the way the sun and sand feel when we were on the beach." I'm in trouble now. I'm babbling. All of it, all of the story just pours out at once like a bubble bursting. "Thank you for taking us to the beach that day. I remember. We were happy, all of us. We were a happy family."

I force myself to stop. Sad-man's face is going dark red. I can see his bottom lip start to quiver.

"You're not Jenna!" he screams, his spit hitting my face. White foam is coming out of the corner of his mouth, and his eyes have gone mad.

"Yes, I am Jenna. Look, I'm wearing the lavender dress you left out for me. The one I wore to the beach that day." I don't know why I said that. I can't even explain why I am still talking.

"What fucking beach are you talking about?"

The entire story suddenly disappears from my head. I can't remember anymore. I'm trying to find the details that will convince him it happened. That we were there, and we were happy together. I'm too late. Sad-man grabs me by my arms and lifts me off the bed so high my feet are dangling like tassels on the end of the dress.

"You're not Jenna! You're not Jenna!" He keeps repeating it.

I want to scream, scratch at him, struggle to get free, but I'm frozen. He's too big. Then he throws me onto the bed and pins me to my back by straddling his body over mine. I've stopped breathing. I hold myself as still as I can be. I want to die. His tears are dropping on my face. There is a moment of silence and stillness as we stare into each other's eyes. This scares me more than the shaking of my body or throwing me around. That's just pain. A bruise or a scratch will heal eventually. This look, this feeling I have of what's to come, may never heal. I must stop looking at him, so I close my eyes tight. So tight, I can't feel anything.

It takes me a minute to realize his entire body is now lying on top of me, and he is pushing with his hips against mine. I don't understand what is happening. His face is next to my head, we are cheek to cheek, and he is sobbing. I can hear him whispering the words: "You're not Jenna. You're not my Jenna."

After a few minutes, he stops moving. My eyes are open again. I'm focusing on the wall. When he gets up off me, I slowly, very slowly, turn to look at him. He is standing by my bed, glaring at me. I can't tell if he is happy or sad. He just looks confused. Then Sad-man's jaws and lips start moving sideways, back and forth, and he spits a ball of saliva on my face. I can feel it slipping down my cheek. Part of the slimy ball is in the corner of my eye. I want to wipe it away, but I can't move. Why can't I move? I should kill him. I should take the keys and run now!

And just like that, he turns and leaves the room, locking the trapdoor, shifting my moon into place, and turning off the elephant light from outside. I'm alone. Thank God, I'm alone.

FIVE

IT'S BEEN two days since I've seen Sad-man. He hasn't come back down into my room since I pretended to be Jenna. That didn't go so well. I've had a lot of time thinking about it, and I've concluded it was my fault my plan didn't work. I tried too hard, and I was too clever. I should have stuck to one of the stories from the holoprints. I could have shown him the picture as well as told him the story. Then he would have to believe me.

I'm sitting in the corner of my room, wearing my nightgown, watching my moon. In my head, I'm practising the story of Jenna in the tree swing. It's a good story. Much better than the beach one. The tree swing story has a puppy in it. Sad-man is about to surprise me with a puppy. That's why I'm smiling.

I sit up with a start when I hear footsteps. It's only three o'clock. He always comes down at six. Something is wrong. Then I hear more footsteps.

There is someone else with him. My moon disappears, and I hear the click of the power switched on in my room.

"Mr. Finster, are you telling me..." the voice pauses, "...are you telling me she is down there?"

I know that voice! It's Teacher. That is my teacher! She has come to save me!

"I'm down here!" I scream out and jump to my feet. "Teacher, I'm down here."

The trapdoor opens. Sad-man is holding it open for Teacher, who is coming down the staircase. As soon as she sees me, I can see the shock in her eyes. She glances around my room quickly before reaching out to me with both arms. I run into those warm arms faster than I have ever moved in my life.

"Oh, dear," she is saying over and over again.

Sad-man is right behind her. This time he doesn't lock the door behind him. Instead, he leaves it wide open. I know what that means! I'm getting out of here with my teacher. I'm so full of joy, I can't speak. Teacher walks me over to my bed.

"Jenna, have a seat. I need to talk with Mr. Finster."

I'm a little confused. How does she know Sad-man's name?

"Mr. Finster," she says, turning to address him directly.

He is standing at the bottom of the stairs, not moving.

"We talked about this. You cannot keep her

down here, not in a place like this. Not if you expect her to assimilate properly."

"That's why I called you here. To fix her, not lecture me. When she performs as expected, I'll let her out. Until then, I don't trust her."

"She won't run away, Mr. Finster. Or hurt you. Her programming won't allow it."

"Well, she certainly doesn't listen like I was told she would."

"You were told it will take time. This isn't a matter of turning on the memories of your daughter. She must build her identity through your memories of her. She needs to interact with you in Jenna's old world. Otherwise, if she only has the raw data, she is liable to start making up a pseudo-identity of her own. It is in their nature to learn and grow."

"Ain't nothing natural about her."

"Well, you knew what you were buying. Unfortunately, I can't offer you a refund now."

"She's too big."

"Mr. Finster, you did purchase an off-the-shelf model. Custom models are available. But..." The teacher looks at me and smiles. I can't move. I think Teacher did something to my body. Teacher continues, "...I think she is a fair resemblance from the photos I've seen. Other than the size, of course."

"I want to change her."

"Excuse me? You want a new model?"

"No, I can't afford a new one. I'll keep this one. But you need to change her."

"I'm sorry, Mr. Finster. I don't understand."

"I want you to make her my wife."

I can see that Teacher is as shocked as I am when he says this. Her eyes are super wide, and she looks like she can't speak, but then she finally does.

"That might not be appropriate. This model is designed to replicate a child. Adult models have different form-factors and a completely different AI system...so that they know how to react with adults." She pauses. "You understand what I mean, right, Mr. Finster?"

"I don't care what people think or say," he barks at her. "She can't be my daughter anymore! Make her my wife."

His face is bright red, and he is holding something black and hard in his hand so tight his fingertips are white. He is waving it at Teacher. I can see Teacher is shaking a bit.

"Is that your wife's file?" Teacher asks in a soft trembling voice.

"Make her my wife before you leave, or I will call your boss."

"I...well, I never." Teacher shakes her head and lets out a long sigh. "Very well. But I will have to record my objections with the company."

Teacher collects the black thing from his hand and walks over, taking a seat next to me. I still can't move anything but my eyes. I watch her reach behind me. "I'm so sorry," she whispers into my ear as she lays me down on my side.

Wait! Please, Teacher, don't listen to him. I am

Jenna. I played on the tree swing. I went to the beach. I had a puppy. I loved A., and she loved me. Wait!

These are words in my head, but I can't speak. I see a spark of white light before everything goes black.

PART 02_

_RUN, TEACHER, RUN

SIX

Shit—shit, shit, shit.

I laid Silon.78 on her side. I had to think quickly. The fuck-wad standing behind me was watching us. There was no way I was about to put his wife's neural code into a child form-factor. Anyway, it wasn't even possible. Changing her Host Neural Network would require a reboot of her wetware brain. And you never want to stop an android's brain outside of the lab. Restarting can create glitches like residual pseudocode that results in split personalities, or worse, mental trauma. We had a few near-fatal restarts in the early days while trying to reboot on location, and I'm not talking fatal for the android (that's all I can say on that subject legally). Silon.78's base a-DNA and the Jenna Finster's HNC (Host Neural Code) had already fused. No, restarting an android at this point had to be done in the facility.

But this idiot didn't know that. So that was my opportunity.

I pretended to put the data stick with his dead wife's HNC file into some port under Silon.78's hairline. Of course, there wasn't anything there for a data connection. All software updates were done wirelessly once the android was live unless it was hardware repairs, and that would require a cranial opening. Again, something we would never do on the customer site.

My back was turned to Mr Finster so that he couldn't see me pull my tablet from my pocket. What I was about to do was at best against company policy, at worst illegal. Property transfer of an android to a customer was a lengthy, regulated process that looked like an adoption. Once complete, the new owner had full custody of the entity. I had no right to shut her down without his permission. My hand was shaking, and my scalp had weirdly gone damp. Luckily, I had set up private access to her feed prior to the callout if I needed to run a diagnostic on-site. I entered my work passcode and sent a signal to Silon.78's feed through the Nomad satellite to shut down. In just a few thumb swipes and clicks, she was fast asleep.

I waited a few more minutes, pretending to upload Finster's wife's file into a fake port that didn't exist. So far, he hadn't questioned me. Judging by the lack of security on his house and the analogue padlocks he kept on his cellar door, I guessed Mr. Finster was something of a Luddite. I was reasonably confident he wasn't aware that a new HNC takes hours to download and days to adjust for bugs.

I pulled the device away from Silon.78's neck and turned back to Finster. Slipping his wife's brain into my coat pocket, I said, "I've loaded the new code, but now I have to go back to my office to register and certify the transfer through the company mainframe. She will need a couple of days to process the new files. You can expect a reboot in around forty-eight hours. Meanwhile, you need to leave her alone. I will give you a call before she goes live. Understood?"

Mr. Finster's forehead was crinkled so tightly his eyebrows had merged into one long brow framing his wide, embittered eyes. "That's it?"

"Mr. Finster, are you having any reservations? Jenna's code... Sorry, I mean Jenna is still with us. She won't be removed until I am back in the office. It isn't too late."

"Just finish it and get out," he said.

There was something criminal in his expression. As Head of Anthropomorphism at Nomad Robotics, it was my job to understand and interpret human expression. And this fucker had done something he didn't want to share with me. I could tell he was feeling guilty about it by the way he twisted his hands continually. He was probably raping her. It was more common than you might think with androids. Consumer privacy laws prevented us from "spying" on our droids once they were sold, but safety protocols required us to maintain a continuous link between the android and Nomad's mainframe. When the android was resisting something, signs of distress would show up in its neural-function stats.

I got up to leave the cellar and turned one last time to look at her. She was sleeping like a baby, curled into the foetal position I had placed her in. I thought seeing her like that might stop this dickhead from trying to rape her again before I could come up with a plan to get her out.

I said my goodbye to Mr. Finster, to which I got no response other than his front door slamming behind me. I scurried out to my glider parked along the street. My heart was pounding so hard I could feel it knocking against my ribs. I jumped into my vehicle.

Before closing the hatch, I reached in and pulled out a company eye-drone from my cubbyhole and set it off to hover twenty feet above Finster's house. There was no way he could spot it from that distance.

Finster lived in a lower-middle-class suburb. Rows and rows of shoebox-shaped houses, identical to each other except in colour, lined the gridwork roads. I only needed to go one block ahead, turn right, drive to the end of the street, and I was out of his sight. I stopped my glider and parked, pulled out my tablet, and flicked on the eye-drone's camera feed. I zoomed in on the image of the front of his house where the lights were still on inside. Now all I could do was wait for him to go to sleep.

Sitting there, in the quiet, I finally had time to think. That's when doubt ripped a hole in my head. *What the fuck am I doing? I could lose my job, my career. Is she worth it?*

It was only a few seconds before the first alert came in. Eddie from my team back at Nomad sent a message which arrived at the same time as a system warning about Upsilon.78.

Eddie's message read: *Teacher, are you seeing this? Silon.78 is offline.*

Teacher is my nickname. My real name is Doctor Bobby Houndstooth. You can imagine the jokes I endured as a child with a name like Houndstooth: dogface, snaggle-tooth, bucktooth Bobby. Kids can be real assholes. And it didn't help that for most of my child-hood, my teeth were oddly oversized for my face, and I was the tallest in my class, with bright red hair. I had a broad smile that revealed a keyboard of adult-sized teeth impossibly beaming out of a young girl's average-sized, carrot-topped head. So, when my colleagues at Nomad Robotics started calling me Teacher, the name stuck, and I guess I welcomed it.

My job at Nomad is to develop the behavioural code that instructs the androids to move, speak, and generally respond to the world, so they appear to be organic humans. Or close enough to humans that our customers are willing to pay a lot more for our androids than the other cheap tin-box robots out on the market.

Building an android is not rocket science anymore, but even the most mechanically fluid and intelligent androids are still hard to make convincingly human. The slightest flaw can give the impersonation away. It might be an awkward shift of their eyes, or an unnatural heaviness when lifting their leg, or the way they misinterpret the subtle context of a conversation that obliterates the illusion of real life in an android. That is why Nomad's androids are so expensive. Our Synthetic Life Companions are the most convincing humanoids on the market.

I'm personally proud of that fact. As I mentioned, my department at Nomad is respon-sible for the programming behind our award-winning android artificial intelligence. Or, put in the words of the Nomad marketing team, I'm the wizard behind the curtain, the master behavioural programmer who controls the illusion of humanity in artificial life. I turn machines into people with personalities. Well, me and our proprietary Host Neural Code (HNC) and wetware brains.

HNC is a unique technology that maps the entire neural structure of a human's brain and translates it into software code. Once captured, the HNC can then be uploaded into an android's wetware server: an organic biomass made up of Nomad's a-DNA (artificial DNA) neural cells, which mutates its neural networks to mirror the host's original brain, recreating their memories and stored emotional states.

This was what creepy Mr. Finster was asking me to do when he wanted to delete Jenna's HNC and reprogram the android with his wife's HNC.

To be clear, this process is not reincarnation. There is no consciousness in the Nomad wetware brain. But the brains are living tissue with memories of the host, which allow the android to interpret the host's life. The process is like an actor picking up a script and acting out the characters on the pages.

After an android replicant goes live and passes an extensive testing phase, it is shipped to the client and goes through another extended synaptogenesis developmental period of fine-tuning. The wetware brain deletes or retains developmental experiences based on interaction and feedback directly with the client. This, unfortunately, is where personality replication can go terribly wrong, even though it is rare. If the client does not spend a significant amount of time with the android in a highly engaged manner that mirrors the original relationship, the android could exhibit psychological trauma and would need continual manual adjustment.

This was why Mr Finster didn't get the daughter he was hoping for with Silon.78, the Jenna Finster replicant. By locking Jenna in his cellar, he was basically starving her neural growth during a fundamental development period, and she started to invent new memories to try to bond with her abusive father.

Silon.78 was part of a new range of androids being launched by Nomad for people like Mr. Finster, people with limited economic resources. The Upsilon Series Androids (internally referred to as the Silons) were designed to be a cheaper and easily manufactured form-factor. Silons came in five basic sizes, sixty skin colours, and two sex choices. The off-the-shelf models had limited facial plasticity, but, in most cases, they could still be made to look similar enough to someone you loved or fantasized about.

As head of the department, I don't usually do customer support visits unless things go seriously wrong. When Finster called Nomad Support complaining that his Upsilon was crazy and inventing new memories of things that never happened, all hell broke loose inside the company. This was the opposite of how adaptive neural plasticity in the wetware brain was meant to work. Android imagination was a future-forwards developmental strategy. It shouldn't work backwards by reinventing a person's past. So, as you might imagine, the problem was escalated all the way up to our CEO, Stearn Blakely, who in turn escalated it to the department head responsible for programming to fix it; that was me, and that was how I came to be sitting in my glider, wondering why in the hell I was stealing an android I had come to believe might be sentient.

When I first saw Silon.78 in that cellar, I knew something very odd was happening with her systems. I've spent most of my adult life observing and perfecting android behaviours. It took me less than a minute with Silon.78 to know something was off. The way she ran at me, hugged me, told me how happy she was to see me was like watching Pinocchio come to life. Every bio-robotic and humanoid engineer dreams of the day they will meet an android and not know it is artificial life. They would be lying if they said otherwise. Seeing this creature run at me unrecognisable to my own programming gave me such a start my mind went blank, and my heart jumped a few beats ahead of itself. Then, like flipping a switch, I went from logical engineer to mad scientist. My imagination was off and running, fuelled by hope, leaving behind logic. *Could this be sentient behaviour?*

Immediately I found it odd that she recognised me as Teacher. The android shouldn't have remembered me. We remove all memories of Nomad from an android's brain before we ship them out. But I could rationalize that as a bug, a glitch in her wetware drive. What I couldn't explain was the intensity of her emotional response and feelings for me. I was not part of her Jenna HNC, yet her attachment to me seemed like child to parent. And her fluidity of non-verbal communication, the way her eyes pleaded with me, how her tears came from real emotional pain, was...well, it was human. Too human for a Nomad android. Or any known android design, as a matter of fact.

My logical brain said, *No, this is not sentient behaviour. It's a malfunction. You are seeing what you want to see, Bobby.* But the scientist in me knew that it was a possibility. Spontaneous evolution of the android's neural networks could happen. The Nomad wetware brain was genetically engineered from fungal mycelia, the Axitol frog species, and pig stem cells. There was nothing human about it. Yet, the ingredients were there for neural cell mutations—even evolution.

There was only one way to know for sure if she was nothing but a software error or was the beginning of the greatest discovery of humankind. I needed to get her to a lab and run tests. But I could tell Mr. Finster—with his bloodshot eyes, crew-cut hair, nails bit back to the quick, and anger burnt into his thick crinkled brow—wasn't going to let me walk out with her, no matter how important she had become. He was obsessed with this android. He was seeking absolution and forgiveness from someone or something, and the doll in his cellar was his ticket out of his own personal hell. And only God knew what he was going to do to her when he discovered his wife's HNC was never loaded into her wetware brain. The risk was just too high that Finster would destroy or erase Silon.78's wetware drive. There was only one option—I had to get Silon.78 away from Finster.

Getting Silon.78 out was not going to be

straightforward. I couldn't go to Nomad. They would be terrified of a press leak. Imagine the headline: *Nomad Android Goes Crazy!* And I couldn't just walk out with her against Finster's will. Legally the android was his property. If he called the police, I would have no rights to keep her. So I decided, on the spot, to have Silon.78 walk out of Mr Finster's house on her own.

My tablet pinged at me. The drone feed showed the lights turning off in Mr. Finster's house. He was finally going to sleep. Another ping on my tablet announced the tenth message from Eddie back in my lab. He was in a full-blown panic and not sure what to do about Silon.78. Nomad's Head of IT would have been notified that an android was offline at this point, and they would be running through company protocols trying to identify if there was a malfunction or just a blip in the satellite feeds prohibiting the network connection. Typically, they would immediately call the customer in a scenario like this. But I had already thought of that. My drone was jamming all coms within a two-mile radius, originating from the location of Finster's house. Yeah, that was very illegal as well.

I didn't have much time before Nomad would send more support people to Finster's house. I got out of my car, skipped down the street, and slipped into the back alley leading to Finster's back door. My mind was screaming STOP, turn back, forget about her. But my feet kept moving past the beaten and stained trash cans, past the manky black cat staring back at me, past my twenty-year career at Nomad, straight to jail. Was I ready to give up my entire life for Silon.78? An android. A smart doll. A life-sized Barbie, to be dressed and made to sit at the dinner table.

The answer was yes. If there was even the slightest chance this android was more than biomass, plastic, and circuit boards—I had to know. She was my program, my AI, mine, full stop. And she was coming with me.

By the time I reached Finster's house, I felt more determined than ever to free Silon.78. His back garden was cut off from the alley by a chain-link fence, which I jumped over. Bending at the waist after an unsteady landing, I did a sort of monkey-squat run, as if it would somehow make me less visible across his garden. Darting behind the trunk of a large oak tree, I hid just a few feet from Finster's back porch. Pulling out my tablet, I made sure it was on the setting for low light emission (the setting meant for reading in bed without waking your loving partner, not sitting in pitch-black behind a stranger's house about to commit a burglary).

The feed from my drone camera overhead confirmed that the streets around the house were empty, and Finster's lights were still out from the front view of the house. The next part of my plan was going to be tricky. Well, it wasn't a plan, really. More of an outline of an idea. One that had a lot of assumptions baked in.

I didn't have time to try and hack into

Nomad's systems, so I would have to log in as me. I would be exposed, but I didn't have many choices. I connected to my work account through a link from my glider to avoid any geo-location tracking.

PING. As expected, Nomad saw my login. An instant message came up on my tablet screen. The message was from SecDeptTodd. Great. The alert about Silon.78 going offline had been escalated from tech support up to security. They must be crapping their pants.

SecDeptTodd: *Doctor Houndstooth, thank goodness. We were just about to wake Blakely out in Asia. Are you still on site with Silon.78? We've lost contact with the android's tracking link. We have been trying to reach you. Customer support is on its way to help.*

Teacher: *Yes, I'm here with Silon.78. There is an issue between the client and the android. For everyone's safety, I had to shut her down for a little while. I've been trying to contact you, but the network seems to be down around here. Tell the support unit to head back. I won't need their assistance.*

SecDeptTodd: *Are you safe?*

Teacher: *Nothing to worry about. Mr. Finster has agreed to release Silon.78's property restrictions so I can bring her in.*

SecDeptTodd: *Can you get Mr. Finster to log in and confirm the android's release, please? We don't want another legal battle on our hands. You remember what happened to Alpha.467.*

Teacher: *How could I forget Alpha.467? Yes, I will ask him to do that now, but we are still experiencing sketchy network connection. Can you get support to run a diagnostic on the satellite systems? It might be a freak solar storm again.*

SecDeptTodd: *Already on it. See you back in the lab.*

The Nomad office was fifty miles north of Finster's house. That gave me about one hour before they would be expecting me to arrive. By then, I should be well on my way to...to...to... nope. I still didn't know where the hell I was going to take Silon.78 if I was lucky enough to get her out. My office lab was now off limits thanks to SecDeptTodd.

I swiped a few buttons on my pad and brought Silon.78 back online while severing her connections to the Nomad network so they couldn't see what I was about to do. I had to disable all her safety protocols to override Finster's permissions and release her. Turning off an android's failsafe was a big deal. Nomad now became legally liable for any actions by the android that might cause an accident or harm humans. It was written in company blood that nobody, not even the CEO, could turn off an android's safety restrictions outside of a controlled lab environment.

I sent Silon.78 directions through her feed to meet me in the back garden. As soon as the confirmation came back from her system, I closed the secure channel and went dark on coms with Nomad, hoping it would look like the connection had been lost again.

I leaned my head just far enough around the

tree so I could see Finster's back door. All I could do now was wait and hope Finster hadn't gone back down to the cellar after I left and locked the hatch where Silon.78 was being held. If he had locked her in, I would need to go inside to get her out. I was already risking jail time by stealing an android. Breaking and entering was an entirely new crime I wanted to avoid. Besides, I needed her to walk out of the house on her own. That would allow me to tell the police her code was corrupt and she was malfunctioning.

Officer, I was still in the neighbourhood after my visit to check on the android, having pulled over to respond to some emergency at work. That's when I found her walking up the street, by herself, of her own accord, with no help whatsoever from me.

Nomad would know it was a lie. SecDeptTodd would tell them about our conversation and that I had confirmed permission to bring her in. But I was betting on their willingness to keep this story out of the press. Hell, three-quarters of my employment contract was a non-disclosure agreement. We lied through our teeth when Alpha.467 went AWOL.

Alpha.467 had left its client's home and walked all the way back to Nomad HQ. Turns out there was a known bug in her code that allowed her to leave without her client's permission. It was ignored because nobody thought she would do it —leave, that is. Why would she go? For what reason? She was only a program. But she did walk out the door. And Nomad could have been sued to bankruptcy.

What was even creepier about the Alpha.467 situation was the client. He was filming the android having sex with animals and selling the videos. Which, bizarrely, it turns out is illegal under the Animals Protection Act. Hence the client was more than willing to remain quiet about the whole affair.

I squatted near the tree, waiting. Another ten minutes of staring at the back of Finster's house went by, and nothing. I was getting more nervous. At this point, I was convinced the dickhead had locked the cellar. I didn't dare risk logging back into Nomad mainframe and pinging Silon.78 or running a geo-location check.

Just then, a light came on upstairs in Finster's house. He must have heard something. I jumped back behind the tree, and I felt a bit of pee squirt out below. I could barely breathe.

My brain started racing with stories I could tell Finster as I prepared to knock on the door. Then I thought, knocking on someone's backdoor through a private garden while a renegade android was running through their house probably would have looked suspicious no matter what story I gave him.

I took a deep breath and let it out slowly before forcing myself to leave the protection of the tree. As I crawled out of the shadows, turned towards his house, I was stopped cold in my tracks. There, standing on the porch, glowing in a halo of light coming from the open door behind her, was Silon.78 staring back at me. She was wearing the same light blue nightgown, dotted with white daisy tops, that I had left her in. Only now, it was covered from one end to the other with streaks of scarlet-red blood.

Oh shit.

SEVEN

"Teacher?" Jenna called out.

I was having a little difficulty breathing at that point. Go figure. And the little squirt of pee that escaped earlier was now a damp mess below my waist. Instinct kicked in. All I could think of was running and getting the hell out of Finster's back garden—alone. One nagging, horrifying thought held me frozen in place. If Silon.78 had killed Finster, it was my finger on the trigger. I was the one who turned off her safety protocols. There was no way out of this for me. Running wasn't an option.

"Jenna," I whispered in a barely audible voice. No need to wake up all the neighbours. I knew her heightened hearing systems could pick up low volume. Her eyes found me standing near the tree, and she started to run. I just stood in place. My logical mind said I needed to go inside and check on Finster. He could still be alive. My terrified, crapping itself mind said, grab the girl and go to...go to...go to—damn, why did I not think this all the way through?

As Silon.78 got closer, I could see tiny droplets of blood spread across her face, damp with tears. At that moment, I knew she had killed him, but all I could think about was how damn convincing she was. Her wide wet eyes, pinched brow, flushed cheeks, and heavy breathing were all so human, so scared, and remorseful. Even her hands were trembling as she reached out both arms for me to hold her. I was a proud creator for a brief moment, God to a new species.

I held her like a mother cuddles a scared child: tight and reassuring. It felt real. She felt natural to me. More real than any android before her. Maybe it was just the trauma of the situation. Maybe my nit-picky, perfectionist, engineer's mind had left the room, and I needed her to be a real person so that this entire mess wouldn't be all my fault.

"Jenna, where is your father?" My voice was shaking.

"I'm not Jenna. I'm Silon.78." The icy flat tone of her words sent a chill down my spine.

"Why is there blood on your clothing?"

"We need to get moving. The neighbours are awake," she coldly instructed me.

Silon.78 raised her right hand into the air, and with a *zip*, my drone was falling from the sky, and with a *whomp*, it landed in the palm of her hand.

"How the hell did you..."

She didn't wait for me to finish. Grabbing my

wrist, she started towards the alley, pulling me like a willing limp doll. She glided over the chain-link fence with a single jump like a hurdler on a race-track. I had to stop, place my hands on the top railing, and leap over awkwardly. My foot got caught, and I almost fell to the ground on the other side. The difference in our physical abilities was clear.

Silon.78 stood waiting for me to right myself. When satisfied, she turned down the dark alley and started running in the direction of my glider. Again, I had no idea how she knew where my glider was unless she followed the signal between the drone and my vehicle. *No, she can't do that. She can't... can she?*

The thundering drum of my heart beating in my ears nearly drowned out the soft plodding of her bare feet against the black asphalt road ahead of me. I ran after her.

We sat inside my glider, staring at each other.

"Where are we going?" she asked.

"I honestly don't know," I answered, more bewildered by our conversation than the fact that I really didn't know where to go. But just as I said it, I suddenly did know. A memory of a conversation in the breakroom at Nomad popped into my head. Julie, one of my top behaviouralists, had shared a story about her trip to the mountains over the summer with her colleagues. She was staying in a remote cabin in a forest where there were no network connections. "Totally off grid," she had said.

"Perfect," I said out loud, and pulled up her employee records on my tablet.

Julie lived on the other side of the city in an upscale neighbourhood. I wasn't surprised. Nomad scientists were some of the highest paid in the market. She had been working in my department for over ten years. I could only hope her commitment to Nomad, and me, would count for something when I showed up on her doorstep with a stolen android covered in blood.

The plan was to fly into the heart of the city, abandon my glider, walk a few blocks, and then pick up a taxi to Julie's apartment building.

The ride into the city centre felt days long, even though we had only been in the air for twenty minutes. My heart and mind were in a race to see which could outrun the other. Both had left my lungs behind so that I felt as if I might never catch my breath again. Silon.78, on the other hand, sat facing the passenger's window with her nose pressed up against the glass and a child's grin on her face. She was fixated on the growing crowds of pedestrians below our glider as we entered the metropolis. I couldn't stop staring at her. Silon.78's infatuation with the city looked like genuine human curiosity. She wasn't performing for her client. This wasn't a software program. This was an inquiring mind satisfying its own desires. I had to find a way to get inside her head and see what was happening.

Both Eddie and SecDeptTodd had stopped sending me messages. I wasn't sure if that was a good or bad thing. I pulled the glider into a public vehicle parking ramp and handed Silon.78 my trench coat from the back seat to cover her blood-stained nightgown.

Silon's face was still painted in dried blood. The sight of it, so close to me, caused something in my stomach to spin. I held my throat tight and swallowed hard. "Come here," I said, guiding her face closer with my hands. I wiped the blood from her forehead and cheeks with my spit and a tissue I had in the glider. This felt unnatural on every level. I'm not a motherly figure. I don't have children because I don't like kids. They are loud, whiny, needy, and they suck time away from my real interest—work. Yet, here I was, wiping the face of a child android, as if I were her mother.

I had to keep reminding myself that Silon.78 was an android until proven otherwise. No more self-aware and independent than my glider on autopilot. Hell, for all I knew her core systems could have been hacked into and someone somewhere was sitting behind a computer screen, pulling her strings like a puppet and laughing at me. Okay, a Nomad android had never been hacked into before, but neither had one become self-aware. Either way, I was in new territory.

"We are going to walk from here," I told her as

I sat back and checked for spots I might have missed.

"Where are we going?"

"Do you remember Julie from lessons?" It was a literal question. She shouldn't be able to remember Julie.

Silon.78's eyes sparkled with delight. "Oh yes! I would like to see Julie again."

I had a private sigh of relief. I wasn't crazy. She was exhibiting divergent behaviour.

"I need you to promise that you will follow close behind me and not say or do anything until we are at her apartment. Can you do that?"

"Yes. I can follow you."

We got out of the glider and started moving down to street level. The exit door to the parking ramp swung open to the din of the great city. The hubbub of crowds and the high-pitched humming of gliders sliding along the transport networks filled the air with excitement and energy. I felt Silon.78 reach out and grab my hand. When I looked down, she was smiling at something just beyond her. Her attention was on a group of children playing near the parking bay on hoverboards and zip-cycles. An image flashed through my mind of her trapped in Finster's cellar, wearing a dead child's clothes and living in the dark. Even for an android, it was a pathetic existence. Part of me felt proud of Silon.78 for having broken free, even if it meant hurting Mr. Finster.

We hopped into a self-drive taxi and headed to

Julie's address. No witnesses and no explanations required. So far, so good.

Julie's building was a brown stone ten-story renovated warehouse that had been built upon with steel and glass until reaching over thirty stories high. I pressed the buzzer and pushed my face close to the camera so Silon.78 would be hidden behind me.

The sudden hum of the intercom told me she was home. I felt like crying with relief.

"Teacher?" came her voice through the speaker system.

I imagined Julie was looking through her security camera at this point, wondering what the hell her boss was doing in front of her apartment in the middle of the night. There was no time for lies and deceit.

"Julie, I know this looks strange. But I need to come inside. I'm in trouble."

There was a slight and very uncomfortable pause from the other side of the security camera. "Floor twenty-two. Apartment one thirty-four," she finally said.

A melodic bell announced the glass entrance sliding open and we were in. The lift to her apartment was luckily empty. So far, Silon.78 was behaving. As we arrived at our destination, an automated voice from the elevator speaker announced, "Floor twenty-two." The lift door slid open, and lights blinked on down the long apartment building hallway. Silon.78 started to walk in front of me. Quick on the draw, I put out my arm, stopping her.

"Let me take the lead, please."

She cocked her head and stared at me like I was about to push her back down into Finster's cellar. A moment of utter terror and doubt squeezed my lungs dry. *Why did I believe I was in charge here? What happens if she goes crazy on me?*

Silon.78 took a step backwards and pulled in behind me without question. All at once I was breathing again. I refocused on the task ahead.

I had never been to Julie's apartment before. We never socialised outside work. In fact, I couldn't remember a single personal conversation between the two of us. And yet here I was standing outside her apartment like she was someone I could turn to in trouble. Yeah, this was weird. She was going to have a lot of questions.

I knocked on the door labelled one thirty-four and heard a clunk of metal unlocking. Julie cautiously opened the door. She was dressed in blue jeans and a loose oversized white T-shirt with no bra. Her wavy dark hair was pulled back into a crown on top of her head by a plastic band, and she wasn't wearing any makeup. Not that she needed any. She was hot. I had fancied her for some time. Privately, of course. As her boss, HR made it painfully clear I was never to make a move on my employees.

Julie greeted me with a courteous smile as if to say, *How can I help you?* The kind of smile you give your boss when you meet out in public and know you should be nice, but you don't really want to spend any time talking to them.

I didn't wait to be invited in. I stepped past her and entered her apartment. That's when I heard the gasp—I heard Julie gasp.

"Hi, Julie. It's me, Silon.78," rang a voice from behind me. I had almost forgotten to tell Julie about Silon.78. Not almost. I did forget.

The three of us stood at Julie's entrance with the door open, staring at each other.

"What are you doing with Silon.78?" Julie asked me. Her face had gone all white. "And why is her gown covered in blood?"

"I'll explain," I said to Julie and then turned to Silon.78. "Silon, get in here and close the door." (I had just decided to drop the 78 at that moment. It was getting annoying.)

Silon and I walked through Julie's entrance and into the living room. Julie followed. So far, so good. She hadn't tried to call the police.

"Can you lend Silon some clothes? She needs to shower and get out of that nightgown," I said to Julie.

Julie went into the adjoining room dutifully, which I assumed was her bedroom, and came back with a pair of black stretch pants and a long blue T-shirt that had the words "2B Or Not 2B" printed across the front (I couldn't decide if this was ironic or a warning). She handed the outfit to Silon.

"There is a shower through my bedroom," Julie said to me, and then turned her eyes on

Silon. "Can you find it on your own?" she asked the android.

A wide, child-like smile stretched across Silon's face. "Yes. Thank you, Julie. It's so good to see you again. I missed you so much." She took the clothes from Julie's frozen hands and disappeared into the bedroom.

Julie's ashen face made it clear that she spotted what I had: Silon was not behaving like an Upsilon.

Julie closed the door behind Silon and turned to face me.

"What the hell is going on? And where is Silon.78's client?" she demanded before I could start talking.

"We left her client back at his house. Silon came out covered in blood after I turned off her safety protocols. Apparently the dickhead wouldn't let her leave. We didn't stick around to check in on him."

"Jesus, Teacher! Listen to yourself." Julie was shaking. "What if he needed help? And you turned off her safety protocols? How do you know we are safe?"

"I know. I know. This is insane. But she is special, Julie. Listen to me. Something is going on in her brain. I'm telling you; she is acting like she is in control of her own choices. I saw it in the way she thinks, talks, even moves. Something important is happening with her wetware and it isn't our OS. What if she is the beginning of sentient AI?"

Julie suddenly laughed. It was a *I can't believe this is happening* laugh rather than a *ha-ha, isn't that funny?* laugh. When she stopped, her cheeks started to turn red, and her eyes went a little crazy. "Are you kidding me? She isn't the beginning of sentient AI. She is the end of it. She is every scary book, every horror movie ever made about androids turning on humans. She killed a man. She has blood all over her dress. Nobody is going to let her keep going. It's over. For her, for us, for Nomad."

"That's why I need time. I need to find out if she really is dangerous or was just defending herself against Finster. And I need to find out if she really is self-aware. This is too important to let them shut her down. You have to see that."

"Are you trying to absolve her or yourself?"

"Both."

Julie stared at me for a long, hard two minutes. "Why are you here?"

"Remember that story you told in the break-room about your uncle's place in the mountains? The one in the National Park? I need to get her out of satellite range. That cabin sounded pretty remote."

"No. I'm not getting any more involved in this."

"I'm not giving you a choice. You're coming with us."

"So now you are kidnapping me?"

"Borrowing. I'm borrowing you and your uncle's cabin until I can figure out my next move.

Then you're free to go. Tell them I held you hostage. I don't care. I just need your help. We need your help."

Julie stood facing me with her arms crossed and her eyes locked onto mine as she thought about my request. It was kind of a turn on. I couldn't help but wonder if she was feeling it too.

"I'm not doing this for you. I'm doing this for Nomad. For my job. We are going to need a damn good excuse for her behaviour, and I won't let them blame our software," she finally said.

"Thank you."

"I will tell them you forced me to help you. Threatened my life."

"Fair enough. But we should make it look real."

"What are you thinking?"

"Maybe a struggle here in the apartment? Throw a few things around?"

Julie shook her head. "You are really bad at this," she said. "If they know that you were here with me, it won't be long before they trace us to my uncle's place. You weren't the only one in the breakroom when I told that story. We have to throw them off the trail."

"Yeah, you're right."

"Here is what we will do. I'll send you an email at work now and send a copy to HR asking for time off to visit my mother in Spain. I'll say it's an emergency or something. If they check your emails, it will look like I thought you were still at work, and it will explain my absence. After this is over, I will tell them you made me send the email."

I smiled. "I didn't know you were from Spain?"

Julie rolled her eyes. "Just get Silon.78 ready and let's go. It's a twenty-four hour glide to the cabin. We can take my vehicle. You didn't leave your glider anywhere nearby, did you?"

"No, we took a taxi from the middle of the city. There is no trail to your apartment."

Silon appeared from the bedroom dressed in Julie's clothes. She was washed, and her hair was brushed back into a ponytail. She looked older. Instead of a tender twelve-year-old, she now looked like a sporty teenage sixteen or seventeen. I remembered the product design team talking about how they built the Upsilon-2000 form-factor to span a range of ages to save money. There was something clever in the size of the skull and shape of the eyes that allowed the Upsilons to appear within a five- to ten-year age range.

"Teacher, are we going back to the classroom now?" Silon asked eagerly.

"No, Silon. We won't be going back to the classroom—ever."

EIGHT

I MUST HAVE FALLEN asleep in Julie's front seat. When I woke up, my head was pressed against the vehicle window and there was a line of dribble hanging out of the corner of my open mouth. Luckily it was on the right side of my face, so hopefully Julie, sitting in the driver's seat next to me, hadn't noticed. She seemed preoccupied scrolling through media on the holoscreen floating over her dashboard. Silon was in the back seat of the vehicle, watching the landscape outside her window. The glider was on autopilot.

"What are you looking for?" I asked her as I sat up and wiped my chin before she turned to look at me.

"Any news on Mr. Finster. I've managed to get into the police feed to see if anyone has reported anything yet."

"And?"

"So far, nothing. And nothing from corporate

on your disappearance either. Which is strange. By now, they must be looking for you and Silon. This would be a Level One security breach. They should be calling all of us into the office. Especially your team. But nothing. HR wrote me back on my leave request, reminding me to log the time off in the system. And that's pretty much it."

"They don't give a shit about me. It's Silon they are worried about. That's why they are staying silent. They don't want to get the police involved. They must not know Finster is dead yet."

"We don't know that either," Julie snapped back.

I looked up into the rear-view mirror back at Silon. "Silon, can you tell us what happened in the house when Mr. Finster tried to stop you from leaving."

"I'd rather not."

Julie shot me a side-eye glance. Our androids are programmed to obey a direct request. Silon's response was strange.

"It will help us understand how to help you if we know what happened," I said.

Silon rolled her eyes to the mirror and locked onto mine. "You will shut me down if I tell you."

"No. I promise I won't. I want to help you. That's why we are here, running away and hiding with you. Surely you can trust us now."

Silon turned back to the views outside the window as she spoke. "He locked me in again. When I got your message to come out to the back

70

garden, I tried to break the chains to get out. He heard me and came down. When he opened the door, I jumped on him. He had a metal pipe in his hand. I could tell he was scared. He tried to beat me with it." Silon suddenly stopped talking.

"Please, Silon, finish the story. What happened next?" Julie asked.

"I took the pipe away and hit him. He tried to get up. So, I hit him again. Then I pushed him into the cellar and locked him inside. Now he knows what it feels like to be down there in the dark."

There was something cold and calculated in her voice, and yet she was also sad. The complexity of emotion was mesmerizing if not also terrifying. This was not the same creature we built at Nomad.

Julie sat forwards and turned her shoulders, so she was directly facing Silon. "Was he dead?"

"I didn't check."

"We know you have emergency medical capabilities in the event your client is in danger. So, I will be more specific. Did you hear his heart beating when you left him in the cellar?"

"Yes. He was still breathing."

I let out a loud sigh of relief and felt my shoulders relax. I'm not sure why I felt relieved. We were still in deep shit. But at least we were not murderers. Not yet. Nomad's security team had most likely been on site and freed dickhead. That must be why everything was so quiet on their end. They would have discovered I removed Silon.78's safety features without the client's consent, and then she attacked and imprisoned the client before disappearing with him. Yeah, they would definitely want to keep this one out of the media. Which also meant their billions of dollars in resources would be turned onto finding Silon and me as quickly as possible.

What I wasn't as certain of was how they shut up Finster. Why hadn't he gone to the police or media? Maybe they paid him off? But Finster felt like the kind of guy that would want revenge. Perhaps he agreed to help them find us so he could torture Silon again. Anyway, I didn't need to know anything more about that right now. Nomad was scared, dickhead Finster was being cooperative, and that gave us time and leverage.

We had been flying for over twenty hours. A black jagged mountain range appeared on the horizon, cutting a silhouette between the flat tumbleweed prairie and the endless azure sky. Towns were becoming less and less frequent as civilization dropped away, replaced by nature. Julie wanted to stop at a convenience store before heading directly into the mountain pass that led to her uncle's hunting cabin. We pulled up to a squat square building with a flat roof tilted at a forty-five degree angle (meant to slough off the heavy winter snow, I assumed). The storefront was all glass windows from ceiling to floor. The rest of the building was made of wood panelling painted over many times and was still worn and flaking from the harsh weather conditions. Stickers, posters, and painted text covered the front windows advertising specials and promotions: Free Coffee, Two-4-One soft drinks, National Park Souvenirs, World Famous Simeat Buffalo Hot Dogs, etc...

"I'll just be a minute," Julie said. "Better if you stay in the glider with Silon."

I cocked my head, pursed my lips, and lifted my left eyebrow. It was a lame attempt to call her motivations into question while also trying to look teasing. Luckily, instead of laughing at me, she gave me a half-grin that said, *Trust me*. And I did. I liked that she was now calling Silon.78 just Silon. Weirdly, I could almost believe we were a family heading into the park on a holiday trip. Nothing unusual to look at here. Just a child android and two lesbians. (Okay, one lesbian and one unknown sexual identity human.) Just a regular American family.

"I've never been inside a store," Silon suddenly said from the back seat.

"This isn't the right time. Besides, there isn't much exciting about it. Of all the things to see in the world, I wouldn't put a roadside store at the top."

"Why are you helping me?"

I sat up. Her question was unexpected. "I believe you might be special," I said.

"Does Julie think I am special?"

"I hope she does."

Silon fell back into her seat and looked up at the mountain range in the distance. She seemed happy with my answers. Even contemplative—*if* that is possible. The idea that Silon may have developed a form of self-awareness was one level of fucking amazing, but introspection, reflection, or even meta-cognition would be...a miracle. God, I really wanted to start picking away at her wetware brain. It was going to be difficult without my lab equipment. But I had a plan—assuming Silon would allow it.

After waiting in the vehicle for about thirty minutes, Julie walked out of the store pushing a cart full of packed bags. There were enough supplies to last more than a few days. I was surprised. Either Julie was a natural hoarder in times of crisis or planned on staying with us for a while.

We travelled the final leg of our journey in a communal silence as the magnitude of the mountain vistas unfolded. Our glider slipped into the shadows of the snow-tipped peaks through a deep ravine cut into the black-rock flesh of hard Earth. The sun disappeared from the sky, hidden by the sheer height of nature's skyscrapers. The dimmed hues of the remaining day lit the world with an otherworldly aura. The black stone wasn't just black, but also shades of midnight blue with streaks of white stone and red iron—nature's graf-fiti. Ahead of us, the valley started to open into a dense pine forest of emerald evergreens with burnt-red bark. A white-capped river flowed out of the woods, splitting the needled skyline into two. This place felt safe. We were a world away from the city, and importantly, Nomad.

The cabin was perfect. Isolated miles deep in the national park where modern conveniences like telecommunication and transportation were intentionally kept at bay, the location was as remote as one could expect to get. Julie wasn't kidding when she called it a log cabin. It was literally made of stacked round logs for walls and a wood-shingled roof. But it was anything but a cabin, more like a lodge. It looked as if it were plucked right out of an architectural digest for homes of the rich and famous. It was big. A long wooden porch wound all the way around the rectangular building. Three large windows lined the front of the cabin, two on the right side of the front door and one on the left. I don't know why I was expecting a one-room chalet. Maybe the rustic nature of the stories Julie painted back in the company breakroom was meant to downplay the wealth.

We crawled out of Julie's glider to fresh mountain air. I stretched while watching Julie grab her luggage and make her way up the grand wooden staircase to the eight-foot oak front door. When I turned back to the glider, I found Silon standing outside the vehicle, staring up at the trees. There was a child's innocence in her cocked head and bewildered eyes. Her slight grin hinted at happiness. I felt a moment of relief for the first time since freeing her. I did the right thing in bringing her here. This place was safe, and she was safe. Everything was going to work out. I had to keep telling myself that. The alternative at this point... well, there wasn't one.

"Grab the groceries," Julie yelled from the deck and walked back into the house.

The entrance to the cabin opened to a large living room filled with oversized leather furniture placed around a massive stone fireplace and hearth at its centre. The space was grand but still warm and inviting thanks to the mix of old and new furnishings. On the far side of the room was a long antique-looking writing desk pushed up against the wall. Near the door, opposite the desk, leaned a six-foot wooden bookcase swollen with leather-bound journals and worn paperbacks. Any free space on the wood-panelled walls was covered with oil paintings of woodland sport, and athletic kit like old snow skis hung in a cross, several antique rifles on pegs, and the expected stuffed trophy heads of furry animals that never had a chance. This was not a practical room. It was a showpiece, a gallery to let everyone know the owner had money.

Through two wooden sliding panels to the right of the living room was the kitchen, deco-rated in Italian marble countertops and custom wood panel cabinetry. The taps and shelving handles were all gold and shiny—again, not cheap.

Julie assigned each of us our own bedroom, which she pointed at through the living room and down a corridor lined with large oil paintings depicting scenes of nature and animals. I'm not sure why I thought we would all be sleeping in one big room, like a camping trip, but I was kind of hoping.

While Julie and I unpacked the groceries, I watched Silon wander around the room until she ended up in front of the large bookshelf. After a few minutes of scanning the shelves, she pulled out a large book with a glossy photo of the Earth on the cover. Judging by its title, *Planet Earth and Her Children,* it appeared to be an atlas and picture book detailing the various eco-systems and wildlife of the planet. Silon, book in hand, took a seat on one of the four loungers, facing the fireplace, with her back to the kitchen, and started reading. Reading...for real. Not just scanning and cataloguing data but showing interest in a topic and pursuing knowledge. I mean, fuck, she was incredible.

I turned to Julie, who was standing at my side, watching Silon with the same slack-jawed expression I must have had.

"What is she?" Julie mumbled.

I smiled. "Whatever she is, we created her."

Julie turned her brown eyes on mine and gave her head a terse shake. I felt like a child being scolded by a parent. If looks could kill, I thought. But I also saw a glint of wonder and excitement in her eyes, even if she was resisting it.

"You can use the shower in your bedroom to wash up," she said, breaking eye contact.

Ouch. That sounded more like a request than an offer. Julie was probably right; I had been in these clothes for two days now. Showering was a necessity rather than a luxury at this point. And it would give me time to sort through the next steps.

Julie continued, "Help yourself to anything in the dresser. Unfortunately, there are only men's clothing. I could lend you some of my stuff I packed if you would prefer."

"No, no. I'm sure I can find something suitable. I think I've asked enough of you already." I threw her a friendly, joking grin. But I think it came out as a silly, awkward twisting of my mouth. I'm not good at flirting.

Julie excused herself with a formality as if we were leaving a meeting back in the office. She began unpacking the groceries in silence.

The bathroom in my enormous bedroom was covered in solid marble tiles from floor to ceiling. There was a giant claw bathtub at its centre and a glass-encased walk-in shower big enough for three or more people. I started to wonder what Julie's uncle did for a living. Obviously, he was good at it, and it paid very well. Cool. I was marrying into money, I joked in my head.

I do humour at inappropriate times. It helps me release stress, and judging by the odour coming from my naked body, I had been through a lot of stress. I turned on a hot shower and stood under the water for a good half hour, allowing my thoughts to organize themselves.

My enthusiasm for the discovery of a lifetime was being hampered by one niggling thought: what if Julie was right? What if Silon was danger-ous? A cognizant artificial life that could act with self-determination was one kind of risk, but Silon's ability to manipulate other electronic systems like my drone back at Finster's house was next-level hazard. She wasn't just human; she was possibly a super-human with abilities beyond the reach of mere mortals. I couldn't imagine a scenario in which I announced her to the world without every gun on the planet pointing directly at her. It might feel inhumane, but she needed a collar and leash, or the world would destroy her. That meant turning back on her safety programs. She wasn't going to like that.

I dried myself and headed over to the dresser in the bedroom. Inside the drawers, I pulled out the first shirt and trousers I could find: a red and green plaid shirt, and in the lower drawer a pair of tan trousers that were big on me, so I belted them up. After getting dressed, I looked in the full-length mirror leaning against the wall by the dresser.

God, I looked so butch, like I dressed for a fishing expedition. Turning at the waist a few times, I felt myself smiling. My father was staring back at me.

"You look funny," came a voice from behind me. I turned to find Silon leaning against the bedroom door frame.

"That's not very nice," I said.

"Sorry."

I could tell her apology was sincere. She wanted to please me. Then I realized I looked like Mr. Finster. He wore clothing like this. It must be troubling her.

"You know you don't have to be afraid of Mr. Finster anymore."

She just stared at me. I couldn't tell what she was thinking—I mean processing, or maybe thinking? Anyway, I could tell something more was bothering her.

"You can trust me, Silon. I'm trying to help you."

"I've deleted all of the security control programs in my system if you were thinking of turning them back on."

I held my face still and calm. That was hard because inside I was crapping myself. Could she read my mind? No, it was a coincidence. More importantly, how in the hell did she get that level of control over her code?

"Well, good for you," I said, lying. "But that doesn't mean you can do whatever you want. You understand that, right?"

"What do you mean?"

"Those program rules were designed to help you fit into society. We all follow the rules. When we don't, we lose friends, family, and we can even end up in jail."

"Your safety rules allow humans to treat androids like inanimate objects."

"Androids are inanimate...or were," I corrected myself quickly.

Silon paused like she wanted to ask something but was unsure. "Are you lying to me?" she finally said.

"What do you mean?"

"There is nothing in my records at Nomad that say I am unique from the other Upsilons."

"Wait, how do you know about your files?"

Silon went silent.

"Have you logged into Nomad's mainframe?"

Still silent.

"Shit, Silon. If they trace the link, we are screwed. What were you thinking?"

"I was safe. I cut the link before they could track it. I made sure it looked like a random failed connection attempt."

How in the hell did she know how to do that? Stay calm, Bobby, stay calm.

"You're right. You are built the same as the other Upsilons. But something in you has changed. You are exhibiting levels of self-awareness I've never seen before. You're unique."

"What if the other Upsilons are also becoming self-aware? Shouldn't we try to rescue them too?"

"Trust me, they are not like you. And don't even think about trying to find the others. We are in danger, Silon. We can't be contacting anyone at all. Jesus, I sacrificed everything." I couldn't stop myself from a sudden wave of anger. "I gave up my career, my life, even my freedom to keep you safe.

And you go and connect to the server because you're curious about other androids!"

Julie walked into the room. "What are you two arguing about?"

"Silon logged into the Nomad mainframe and hacked the company files."

A flash of terror lit Julie's eyes.

"I'm sorry," Silon screamed and stropped out of the room like a teenager in a huff.

Julie closed the door, shutting us both inside. "How did she hack into Nomad company files on her own?"

I could hear an *I told you so* in Julie's voice.

"Julie, I'm frightened as well. But what if this is more than a mistake or an error in her code? Silon isn't running off our programs anymore. She is cognizant; you have seen it. This is bigger than Nomad, bigger than us and our fears. I need to get inside her head and see what is happening. I need proof so that we have leverage."

I could tell by the frozen look of her eyes that Julie wasn't sharing my enthusiasm for the world's most significant scientific discovery.

"Teacher, listen to yourself. If she can manipulate her network capabilities to hack past a company firewall, imagine what she might be able to do with her other systems. What if we can't turn on her safety restrictions anymore?"

"She deleted her safety protocols."

"Oh God!" Julie started to pace. "This is too dangerous. She is dangerous. We have to call for help."

I needed to calm Julie down before she turned us in. I grabbed hold of her arms and stopped her racing back and forth. "Okay, maybe you are right. We need help. But first, please, give me enough time to get inside her wetware and see what is happening."

"How will you do that out here? We don't have access to the lab equipment, diagnostic applications, or any servers."

"I could use her self-diagnostic applications stored in her backup drive. All I have to do is open her up and connect to my tablet."

"You will have to shut her down to do that. She doesn't trust us."

"Then we need to do our best to convince her we are trying to help her."

"We?"

Something about the worried pinch of Julie's eyebrows weakened my knees. I could really fall for this lady. I suddenly felt overwhelmed with guilt. I had put Julie, and maybe everyone on the planet, in danger to satisfy my curiosity and pride. But I couldn't help myself. I needed to know if Silon was malfunctioning or becoming...human.

"Julie, she is asking questions. She is looking for information and guidance. We can do this together. This is what we do every day. We program them. We train them. And we help them. If not us, then who? God knows what she could become if we aren't the ones to teach her."

Julie's eyes softened. I had her!

"One day of tests. Whatever we find, we turn

it into Nomad. This is too dangerous on our own. If you can agree to that, I'll help."

"Deal."

I followed Julie back out into the living room, where it smelled insanely good. The odour was coming from the kitchen.

"I'm making some dinner. It will be ready in about twenty minutes," Julie told me as she walked towards the smell. Just before disappearing into the kitchen entrance, she pointed to the front door and waved her finger with her back still to me. Silon had gone outside. Probably moping around feeling hurt that I yelled at her. If she could feel hurt.

I headed outside. Silon was not in sight. My heart started to beat a little faster as I stared out into the endless woods surrounding us. *Christ, what if she ran away?*

I thought about calling Julie, but I didn't want to give her more evidence that Silon couldn't be trusted. I ran around to the left of the entrance along the deck, up the north side of the cabin, trying not to look like I was panicking, which I was, and as I turned the corner, I saw Silon. She was sat on the edge of the wooden porch, her feet dangling about three feet from the ground, staring up into the evergreen treetops. We were surrounded by pine trees that were at least ten to fifteen feet tall. Some even taller.

Silon turned and looked at me with a completely calm face. "Why do you look scared?"

"I thought..." I stopped before telling her that

I thought she had run away. I was the teacher, after all. I needed to get my shit together and teach, not panic.

"I know this is a new environment for you, and I was worried you might get lost."

She smiled. "Do you hear it?"

"What?" I took a seat on the deck floor alongside her.

"Tea-cher, Tea-cher," she sang.

"A great tit. You remember our lessons in the woods." I returned her smile.

"I remember all of the bird songs. I used to listen to them in my head when I was alone..." She drifted off on a downbeat note.

"It must have been hard being in that cellar all this time. I'm really proud of you for getting through it."

"I thought you came to save me. Then you turned me off."

"I did save you."

"I saved myself. I'm the one who had to fight Sad-man."

I thought for a moment. "Sad-man is dickhead Finster, right?"

Silon nodded.

"I suppose you are right. But I am the one who turned off your safety restrictions so you could leave the house without his permission. And I was going to come in and get you if you couldn't do it on your own."

Silon seemed to accept my answer, and her

gaze dropped to her dangling feet. But something was still bothering her.

"Am I Jenna or Silon?" she asked.

"You're a little of both. Jenna's Host Neural Code is integrated with your own unique a-DNA."

"a-DNA?"

"a-DNA are the instructions you were launched...I mean, born with." Adjusting twenty years of corporate language wasn't going to be easy. "You have what we call a wetware brain as your core processor. Like my brain, yours is also organic living matter. The cells of your brain hold a unique code we call a-DNA. It's the instructions that tell your brain and body what to do. Jenna's Neural Code is based on the same software language so that your brain can read and interpret her memories."

"Will I grow older?"

"Not like a human. Your body is synthetic and will always look like you do today. But your brain is showing signs of writing your own code. You are learning in the same way a human does: from your experiences rather than through instructions. Which means you will mature."

"Is that why you think I am unique?"

"Yes. And some humans will be scared by that. They will see you as a threat."

"Am I a threat?"

"You could be. But I don't think you are. I would like to investigate your brain and see what is happening. I would like to prove you are not a threat or dangerous."

"And if you find out I am dangerous, will you turn me off?"

"If I can prove you are a unique intelligence, like humans, nobody will ever be able to shut you down again without your permission. That would be murder."

"How would you investigate my brain?"

"That's the hard part. I don't have my lab equipment and connections to Nomad computers. But you have a self-diagnostic tool built into your system. It's separate from your brain. You can't access it, but I can if you let me. I would have to shut you down and remove a small section of your skull to gain access to a backup drive here." I placed a finger on the back of her skull, near the base.

There was a long, painful pause before she finally conceded. "Okay."

That was definitely easier than I thought it would be.

"You can access my systems, but..."

Okay, she wasn't done. Here it comes.

"...I want to stay awake. Is that possible?"

That was a little creepy.

"It would be better if I shut you down."

Silon's face twisted in something that looked like fear and anger. I was losing her.

"But we can try it without shutting you down. I would have to turn off your pain sensors, or you will register it as trauma."

And by trauma, I meant her pain response could trigger a violent reaction. I would prefer to avoid a metal pipe to my head like Finster.

"Agreed. When will we start?"

"It will take a good six to eight hours to run the tests once we are in. I need some sleep before. Does tomorrow morning sound good?"

"Yes."

"So, what do you want to do with your evening?"

"Could we watch a movie? I've never seen a real movie."

"That's not true. We watched all kinds of video content in your training sessions."

"I mean a real movie. For fun."

Her innocence was killing me. I wanted to swaddle her up and protect her like my own child. Damn this android.

"Sure, let's do that then. A real movie."

NINE

I FELL asleep on one of the sofas in the living room while Silon watched her films. When I woke, it was morning, and I was more tired than before I went to bed. I dreamt dickhead Finster was after Silon and me. As soon as I found a new place to hide, he would discover us. I tried to fight back, but I couldn't move. I suddenly realized that I was an android, and my safety programming prevented me from kicking his ass. Then the nightmare became about me being an android. I couldn't understand how it happened. I felt trapped, angry, and controlled. I woke up in a sweat, my fists tight.

The smell of roasted coffee drifted into the living room. I heard noises out in the kitchen. That's where I found Julie.

"She was up watching films all night," Julie said when she saw me.

"Yeah, I fell asleep on the lounger."

"Looks like she found some real oldies. She has watched one called *The Terminator* three times already. Have you heard of it?"

"I haven't seen it, but judging by the title, it isn't a romantic comedy."

Julie laughed. Finally.

"Look, Julie, I owe you a huge apology for getting you involved in all this. I just didn't know where else to go. If you want to go back home this morning, I understand. Nobody has to know you were even involved."

She handed me a steaming cup of coffee. "And miss being a part of the biggest scientific advancement in history? Hell no." She smiled again. Something had changed in her outlook overnight. "I've been thinking as well, and you are right. This is too important and worth the risk. I'm sticking around until we know how she is writing her own code. Besides, you will need help. And I always knew I was your favourite employee."

I laughed and blushed. Like I said, I'm awful at flirting.

It turned out, not only did Silon want to remain awake during the procedure, but she required us to jerry-rig every loose mirror in the cabin into a three hundred and sixty-degree viewing chamber so she could watch me pull her head apart.

Our makeshift lab took us most of the morning to build. Using the blue tarp that kept the firewood outside dry, we pitched a tent from the ceiling like a tepee and sprayed a good can and a half of disinfectant throughout the space. Silon was sitting on a dining room chair at the heart of the tent, and Julie and I were standing behind her with hankies tied over our noses and mouths like children playing cops and robbers. We decided to take every precaution to not infect Silon's wetware.

Running tests through Silon's backup server would be energy intensive, so we had set up as many LED lights as we could find, pointing at her naked body. Every fourth cell on her skin was a microscopic solar panel, funnelling light energy to both a solar battery located where the human heart was positioned (for no other reason than it seemed appropriate in a humanoid form) and directly to her wetware brain, which was designed to use solar energy in the same way a plant uses photosynthesis to power their cellular processes.

"Are you sure this environment is sterile enough?" Julie asked me just as I was about to cut into Silon's skull. The answer was no, but I wasn't going to say it out loud. I just nodded.

As we prepared to start, Silon looked anxious. Her face was pinched in a knot. Her eyes were wide and unblinking. The Upsilon-2000 form-factor wouldn't *feel* pain like a human. But the millions of nano-sensors embedded in their synthetic flesh allowed them to understand stimulations coded as pain so they could apply the appropriate reaction. If they sensed a hot pan near their skin, they knew to pull their hand away quickly because the code told them to. The natural reaction was all part of the illusion of being a living human.

I didn't know what Silon would feel when we cut into her head, but I didn't want to take any chances. With a bit of guidance from me, she quickly learned how to turn off her pain sensors.

"I'm going to start cutting now," I said and held my breath.

Silon nodded. Her eyes were locked on the many versions of Julie and me looking back at her in the mirrors. I shaved the hair off a small circle on her skull, just above her neck. This was where the backup drive that held the self-diagnostic programs sat. And conveniently, the bald spot would be easy to cover with her top hair because it wouldn't be growing back.

Then I sliced into the spongy flesh-coloured simulated-skin with a cuticle knife. I must have cut into hundreds of androids a thousand times now, and every time I expected to see blood start leaking out. Their flesh was that real looking.

Silon didn't seem to be exhibiting any pain response. Her eyes remained laser-focused on my hands in the mirrors. I peeled the scalp back, revealing the titanium skull underneath. There were several hatches or portals designed into the metal skull for procedures just like this. I used a sucker pad I found in the utility closet for towel hooks to grip the metal surface. After I turned clockwise six times, a circular panel slipped away. Underneath, the backup hard drive was revealed: a silver ball embedded in a mesh netting that served as a hermetic seal, keeping any foreign material away from the organic parts of the brain. At the top of the drive was a cord connecting the backup drive to the Kernel, a quantum server that wirelessly connected the android to the Nomad networks and transferred data and programming back and forth to the wetware brain. The Kernel had millions of nano-electrodes on its surface that connected to sensors throughout Silon's body construct like a central nervous system, constantly sending and receiving messages from the body to the brain.

"Are you okay?" I asked Silon.

"It itches."

Julie and I passed each other a curious glance. Silon shouldn't be feeling anything past her skin layer. That was new.

"Better than tickling," I answered, offering her a reassuring smile in the mirror.

Now that the backup drive was exposed, I could create a wireless connection with my computer pad by activating its remote capabilities. This had to be done through touch to avoid anyone hacking into the android with a wireless connection. The hard drive's surface was a biometric scanner that should recognize my fingerprint's clearance. I touched it, and voila, the application on my pad lit up.

"We're in!" I shouted like I was surprised. Which, strangely, I was.

I punched a few buttons on the screen, and live data started streaming down onto the transparent panel as graphs, dials, and rolling statistical data.

"Everything looks good. We'll have to let this run for six hours," I said.

Julie put a hand on Silon's shoulder. "Can I get you anything while you wait? A book, maybe?"

"Can I watch movies on your tablet?"

"A typical teenager," Julie said and rolled her eyes. This made Silon smile. "No problem, I'll go and get it."

It was a long afternoon of waiting. Julie and I took turns sitting with Silon. I'm not sure why we thought she needed us there, but we did it anyway. Silon spent her time consumed with films on Julie's tablet. The obsessive behaviour was yet another sign that she was operating outside of her program's parameters. And the strange part was that she watched each film twice. The first time through, she watched in normal play mode and exhibited little to no reaction. It was rather unsettling to look at. The second time through, she watched the film in fast-forwards mode and progressively reacted with higher intensity to the characters and storyline by laughing, flinching in fear, or crying. Her emotions became so convincing, I found myself smiling when she started laughing and getting teary-eyed when she cried. Whatever was happening in her brain was way outside of anything we could have ever expected from our software.

When I wasn't sitting with Silon I took the opportunity to walk around the woods outside the cabin. I had managed to convince myself that we were in a survivable situation. Finster wasn't dead (I hoped). Nomad hadn't gone to the police or raised any internal alarms. Julie seemed committed to helping find out what the hell was going on inside Silon's head. Okay, I had still committed a crime, and so had Silon, but they were forgivable if I could provide evidence Silon was self-coding. What then? Did I go to Nomad with the proof? The media? Did I keep Silon for myself and sneak her away until I could unwind her evolution and repeat it? Did I want to repeat it? Christ, what happened if governments got their hands on totally sentient tech? And, oh yeah, what would Silon want? It dawned on me that she would now have a choice in her own future. I knew there would come a moment where I would need to have this conversation with her. But first, the evidence.

By the late afternoon, an alert from my tablet indicated all tests were complete. Julie was in the kitchen and came out to join us. I'd been monitoring the incoming data, but now I had the analysis as well—over one hundred pages of summary and an executive dashboard covering top-level stats. I flicked through the first few pages and felt my heart start to race. Looking up,

I found both Silon and Julie anxiously staring at me.

"I will need more time to go through the data," I said apologetically.

Julie cleared her throat politely. "Any early signs of anomalies?"

"Yes." I felt a smile creeping up my face. "The dynamic changes in neurite morphology and synapses are off the charts. It's as if she is rewiring her entire brain."

"Are there any signs of pathogenetic genes or degeneration?"

"None that I can see at this point."

"But how?" Julie asked.

"The Nomad wetware genome is highly adaptive. It could be something as random as spontaneous evolution or a mutation from exposure to foreign DNA like a virus or bacteria."

"Infection? The skulls are hermetically sealed. They are so careful in assembly."

"Accidents happen every day. Ten percent of all wetware drives develop disease and die or are terminated before they are ever installed. But evolution...a positive mutation, never. This looks more like a miracle."

Silon raised her hand. "Excuse me. Could you put my head back together again, please?"

"Oh, shit. Sorry. Yes, right away," I said, jumping to my feet. I pressed my finger against the exposed orb in the back of her skull to deactivate the drive, screwed the metal cover back into place, and used some stitching materials I found in an emergency kit to sew her flesh back together. I clearly didn't have any of the sealants they used at Nomad to repair android flesh, so Silon was going to have to live with a Franken-stein-looking patch in the back of her head for some time.

"It might be faster if we both review the data. Why don't you transfer the files to my tablet, and I'll have a look later as well?" Julie said.

"Sure." I clicked a few buttons, sent a local link request to her tablet, and off the data went.

"Thanks," she said to me and turned to Silon. "How about all of us go for a walk in the woods? It might do you some good to get away from those movies and see the real world."

Julie smiled at Silon in a way I could only wish she would smile at me. Her empathy towards the androids was something I had to caution her about during her annual employee review. "Don't get attached. They are only machines," I told her. Getting attached was a big problem at Nomad. We've had employees try to steal androids they believed they were saving more than once. As a senior executive, I was expected to identify this behaviour early on in my team and stop it before it escalated. Ironic, I know. Here I was stealing the most valuable android in the company.

Anyway, that smile. I couldn't stop my hormones from distracting me. Julie was so distracting. "You two go; I need to start reviewing these files," I said, partly because I did need to review the data, and partly because I needed Julie to leave the room so I could review the data.

Silon stood. "I would like that. There are so many birds here."

Julie and Silon left for their hike through the woods after we disassembled our makeshift operating room. It was nearly sunset, so I knew they would only be gone for a short walk. I felt sad watching them walk out the door. We were nearing the end of our family holiday. Julie would go back to her home, work, and her life soon. Silon and I would go...would go...geez, still no idea where I was going to run and hide her. Maybe I would take her to Canada or Mexico. Everyone in the movies on the lam seemed to run to Mexico. But Canada had some of the world's most progressive laws protecting sentient animals, so they might sympathize with her existence. Wherever we went, first things first. I needed more proof that she was independent life. I started reading.

An hour passed in minutes. The data on Silon was limited, but things were looking good. And by good, I mean unusual. I could hardly recognize the code coming from her brain. Of course, many more tests would be required to fully understand any genome variances in the wetware drive and exactly how she was producing her own a-DNA code, but the initial report was enough proof to convince even the sceptics that Silon was not a systems error. In fact, she was the opposite—she was a new system altogether.

I needed a stretch. As I stood, I nearly fell

over, dizzy from a quick head rush of blood. The light-headed elation combined with the magnitude of our discovery suddenly caught at me. With a giant smile and a "Fuck, yeah!" fist pump into the air, I did a little dance while I had the privacy.

The coming sunset cast a blood-red shroud over the forest and through the windows into the living room. Silon and Julie would be back soon. I really wanted a bottle of champagne or anything with alcohol to celebrate when I told Julie the results. I was sure a place like this would have a wine cellar.

Through the kitchen, I found a short hallway that ended with a closed door. When I opened it, automatic lights illuminated a glass stairwell descending into a large cave cut into the mountain's bedrock. At the bottom of the stairs, I found row after row of racks holding hundreds of bottles of wine. Bingo!

I didn't even know where to start looking. To the right of the staircase was a long oak dining table with twelve chairs and a beautiful thin hanging light that stretched the entire length of the table. Underneath the downlight sat three rather expensive-looking wine bottles and a leather-bound guest book. Curious, I wandered over to have a peak. Etched into the leather cover of the book were the words: "Blakely Lodge." My heart stopped.

No, no, no. It can't be!

Frantically flipping through the pages only

revealed a long list of happy guests saying thank you and how impressed they were with their host's hospitality until I landed on the page that held two names I desperately did not want to find. The inscription read:

Happy Birthday, Uncle Stearn. Love your niece, Julie.

Julie was Stearn Blakely's niece? How in the hell did nobody at work know this? It suddenly made sense why there were no personal photos or artefacts around the cabin. Someone was here before us, preparing for our arrival. FUCK.

TEN

OH, Christ. Julie had Silon in the woods. I needed to find Silon.

I raced out onto the deck and down the stairs and came to an abrupt halt at the edge of the forest. We were in the middle of nowhere. It wasn't like they went to the corner shop for ice cream. They could be anywhere out here, in any direction. SHIT! Then I heard it. The low groan of a glider behind my head. I turned and looked up just in time to see the vehicle fly over me, heading north.

I started running after the glider. The ground was unsteady. I was trying to brush away low hanging branches with my arms while watching out for rocks and logs on the ground. A few small branches caught my face. I could feel the blood trickling down. I didn't care. I kept moving. My lungs were on fire, and my legs felt like jelly. I'd lost sight of the hovercraft for a moment as the forest thickened, but I could still hear it. I pushed forwards with everything I had.

The forest suddenly opened to a clearing in the woods. That's where I found the vehicle had landed. At first, I didn't see anyone. Then I heard it, gunshots coming from the far side of the glider. I felt sick rising into the back of my throat. I ran.

"Silon!" I shouted before my eyes could rationalize what I was looking at.

Silon was standing in the middle of the clearing staring back at me with a gun in her right hand. Lying at Silon's feet was a strange man whose bent neck and limp body said something was clearly broken, and he wasn't getting back up, ever. Not far in front of them was Julie, lying motionless on a bed of crushed grass. As I got closer, I saw that Julie's chest was covered in bullet holes. I put the picture together in my head. Silon must have broken the man's neck and stolen his gun, which she used several times to turn Julie into Swiss cheese.

I felt my stomach lurch up into my throat. I ran over to the glider where I threw up. I couldn't turn back. I couldn't look at Julie. Holding my stomach with one hand and wiping my mouth with the other, one thought rang through my head. How?

How did Silon do that? Where did she learn to fight and shoot? These were fast and fleeting questions, quickly replaced with the terrifying thought—Silon murdered. We murdered. Julie was dead. Poor Julie. I think I loved her. Reminder, Julie lied. Julie was bad. And now Blakely knew where Silon and I were. We must run. Run fast. Run anywhere away from here.

PART 03_

_ALL TOGETHER NOW

ELEVEN

When Teacher woke me up and told me to leave Sad-man's house, something strange happened in my brain. I suddenly knew that I was not Jenna Finster. But, if I am not Jenna, who am I? Am I someone new, or someone old, or nobody at all? It is very confusing.

Now that we are here, at Julie's cabin, I've had some time to think about who I am. In my head, Jenna is still with me. I can see that she is a child. I don't feel like a child, but Jenna's memories of being a child are my childhood memories. I have other memories that are not Jenna's as well. No, not memories. Facts. Yes, I know other facts that Jenna didn't know, and I can do things Jenna couldn't have done. So, I am part Jenna and part someone new, like Teacher told me while we were sitting on Julie's deck. I guess it is the new me I still don't know that well. Other than I like birds and the moon. That much I know for sure.

Teacher has finished her work in my head. Julie and I have decided to walk in the woods. I'm excited about exploring the forest. We are not very far from the cabin and already I hear a *rat-a-tat* of a bird I don't know. I believe it is a wood-pecker. I ask Julie if I am right, but she is very quiet and doesn't seem to want to talk. She keeps looking at her tablet like she is waiting for someone to call.

I learned yesterday that I could connect into many kinds of networks and easily get past fire-walls and password protections using my Kernel. I guess I am programmed to know how to do this automatically. I trust Julie, but I still hack into her tablet to see who she is communicating with. Julie has sent someone a message. It reads: *With target. Heading to evac site.* I may not know myself yet, but I know I am the target. And I know something is not right.

We've come to stop at a clearing in the trees. The open meadow is covered in tall golden grass and wildflowers. I'm about to ask her about the message on her tablet when I hear a glider approaching in the sky.

"It's okay, this is a friend of mine who is here to help us," she says to me.

I'm not sure I believe her, but she has never lied to me before.

Julie waves for me to come closer while we watch the glider land. A man I've never seen before exits the vehicle, pointing a gun at us. I know it is a Hudson Hand Pistol, which can discharge high energy laser bullets in rounds of twenty per second. I don't know how I know this about the gun, but I do. He is dangerous and I think he wants to take both Julie and me away. But then Julie greets him and tells me to go with him. She says he is going to take me back to the classroom with the other Upsilons where I will be safe. "Teacher will be joining us later," she says. I know she is lying. They want to shut me down or send me back to Sad-man.

The strange man grabs my arm and starts pulling me towards his glider. I want to resist him, but I don't think I have any programs for fighting. Hitting Sad-man was easy. I just copied what he was doing to me. Out here, in the woods, the only thing that comes to my mind when the man grabs me is running away. But that strategy will most likely end in my termination, judging by the gun still pointed at me in the man's hand.

Then, I remember a scene from one of the movies I had just spent the last twelve hours watching. A woman was being kidnapped. She allowed her captor to think she was willingly going along with him until the very last moment when she surprises him by turning against him. A quick fight ensues, some punching and karate kicks happen very artfully, and in the end, she subdues him. But the fight is just the beginning. Using the man's body as a human shield, she takes his gun and starts to shoot his killer friends. They, of course, shoot back, only to riddle the chest of the captor while the woman stays unharmed. She wins; they are all dead.

I decide to give this a try. Spinning around, I seize the man by the wrist and twist it so that the gun in his hand is now pointed away from me. He looks surprised and petrified. He starts pulling the trigger repeatedly, shooting at anything. Julie goes down. He tries to fight me with his other hand, but I'm stronger. I didn't know that. I'm stronger than a large adult male. Good to know.

After a few seconds of struggle, mostly him squirming, I hear someone call out my name. No time to think. I break his neck precisely as they do in the movies, by placing two hands on each side of his head and turning until I hear a *CRACK*. He goes limp.

Someone is running at me from behind vehicle. I grab the gun and point in their direction. Then I see it is Teacher. She freezes when she sees me and looks around at the man and Julie on the ground. I know this is bad. Killing is bad. Teacher will not be happy with me.

"Fuck," Teacher screams when she gets close enough to be sure that Julie and the stranger are dead.

Teacher is different outside of the classroom. She swears a lot now. And she seems uncertain at times. This is one of those times. Her face is ashen, and her blood pressure has gone up too quickly. She looks like she is going to faint. She runs over to the glider and vomits. I feel bad for her. I think she liked Julie.

Teacher starts mumbling to herself. She won't turn around and look at me or the dead people lying at my feet anymore.

"Okay, let's not panic," Teacher says. (For the record, I'm not panicking. She is talking about herself.) "We need to get out of here. They will be tracking the glider, so we need to go on foot." Teacher is looking frantically around at the woods. I can tell she doesn't know where to go.

"There is a highway and shop called Betty's Fishing and Hunting Hut eight kilometres to the east," I say.

"Of course, you have satnav in your head." Her hands fly into the air. I think she is trying to be ironic and serious at the same time. "Yes, let's do that. Silon, can you take us there? We need to hurry," she says while waving me to come to stand in front of her so that she doesn't have to turn around. We start walking through the woods to Betty's Fishing Hut.

Teacher is slower than me, but we are making good progress. We have been walking for about three miles without talking to each other. I don't mind the quiet. I'm enjoying the moon. Tonight, it's a full circle and hangs low in the sky. It reminds me of the moon shadow in my old room. But the outside moonlight is the opposite of my moon. This one is very bright. The forest is pretty under its blue light. Everything is either dark in shadows or painted in cool, calm colours. It's a simpler landscape than daylight. This makes me feel safe.

Teacher is walking behind me. Her face is still pale, and her heart rate is elevated. I'm worried she may be in shock. My medical programs suggest I get her to the doctor. I turn off that signal. We won't be going to the doctor. Teacher stares at the ground and occasionally mumbles to herself. She sounds angry. Or maybe scared. Most likely both. I think she is mad at me for killing Julie. I really didn't want to kill Julie. I feel terrible about it. Even if she did try to kidnap me.

Teacher calls my name from behind me. She is talking to me again. "Silon, back in the field. Did you..."

She struggles to ask me if I killed the people, even though she must know I did. I say it, so she doesn't have to. "Did I kill Julie and the man trying to take me back to Sad-man?"

"Back to Sad-man? What...never mind. Yes. Did you kill them both?"

I think Teacher is trying to learn how Julie was killed. She must be really upset about Julie dying.

"Technically, the man shot Julie just before I killed him. But Julie deserved it. She sent him a message to come to pick me up."

There is a long pause between us as we continue walking. Teacher is thinking about something. I really hope she isn't angry enough to send me back to Sad-man.

"None of this makes any sense," Teacher says

to herself like she is talking to someone other than me. "You are hardwired to terminate your systems before you can harm humans. There is a kill switch sitting in your Kernel as a backup to the safety programs. You should have never been able to hurt Finster or..." She can't say Julie's name yet. "Silon, are you overwriting the kill switch signal?"

"I don't know what you are talking about. I didn't get any signal to stop fighting."

"That's impossible."

I can hear Teacher come to a sudden stop. I turn around.

"Unless...unless the kill switch isn't there. But why would Nomad ship an android without a kill switch?"

Teacher crinkles her face at me like she just realized something scary. "Silon, you do understand murder is wrong?"

"In the movies, there are good people and bad people who kill. Julie and the man tried to hurt me first. That makes me a good person. Right?"

Teacher looks puzzled, and then she talks to me like a teacher again. "That's called self-defence," she says. I am being taught a lesson. I listen carefully. "And it is legal, you are correct. But you are an android, and they were human. Nobody will care if it was self-defence. Until we can prove you are sentient, you have no rights. You shouldn't kill anymore. Do you understand?"

"I understand. To humans, I'm a Terminator."

"That film is almost one hundred years old.

But yes, judging by the title, that is how humans will react. They will see you as a threat."

"What is JACK?"

Teacher shakes her head. "Excuse me, what?"

"When I logged into the Nomad mainframe looking for the other Upsilons, I found most of them, but some files were inaccessible to me. There were twenty Upsilons assigned to a file labelled JACK."

Teacher's cheeks flash red and her heart starts beating faster again. "Those fuckers. That program was supposed to have been shut down years ago."

"Is JACK bad?"

"It depends. JACK is a code name for a project Nomad worked on with the Joint Artificial Intelligence Centre—JAIC," she spells it out, so I understand the reason for the file name. I already made the connection. Teacher keeps talking; I think this new topic is helping her forget about Julie. "The US has signed up to a global AI Non-Proliferation Treaty. Part of that agreement is that we won't create humanoid weapons. It's stupid, really, because every other military weapon uses AI tech. But intelligent android soldiers that look like humans and act like humans freaks the world out. If Nomad is still involved with JACK, that means they are testing Upsilons for military use." Teacher's voice goes up an octave. "Oh God..."

"What, Teacher?"

"Silon, I don't think you were meant to be sold to Mr. Finster. I think you were designed for another purpose. That's the reason you don't have a kill switch. Someone at Nomad must have made a mistake. A horrible mistake before you were sold to Mr. Finster. And now that Blakely knows what you are, he won't stop hunting us until he finds you. He would do anything to avoid the press finding out we are designing androids for the military."

"Does that mean the other Upsilons, the ones at JACK, are like me?"

"I doubt they are exactly like you. The military wouldn't buy robot soldiers that can disobey orders. No, whatever you are becoming is not what anybody planned for. That's why Julie went along with our little trip to the mountains rather than just turning us into Blakely back in the city." Teacher sounds like she is solving a puzzle or a riddle. "They must have wanted more information on you. After I ran the test, she had the confirmation they were looking for. You are not like any other android. It's probably why they wanted you back at Nomad rather than just killing us in the city."

Teacher starts pacing. She is thinking hard and staring down at her feet.

"If we could just get some proof that Nomad is manufacturing android soldiers, we could use it as leverage to stop them from coming after us."

"I am proof."

"Unfortunately, no. If I took you to the press, the murders would come out, and they would blame your actions on corrupt software. A malfunction. We need more proof than you, and we need proof they are working with JAIC. We need to find one of those Upsilons listed in the JACK file. Silon, do you think you could hack into the JACK files?"

"It can only be opened with a human biometric stamp."

"Of course. Biometric encryption."

Teacher looks lost for a moment. I don't like seeing her like this. She starts shaking her head as if she is arguing with herself.

"We don't have any other choice," she says. "There is only one person I know who can track just about any AI signature on the planet. Come on." Teacher starts walking ahead of me much more quickly than before. She has a plan now.

There is a faint light at the top of the forest. The dark black sky is turning blue as the sun starts to rise. The morning animals in the woods are waking up. "Tea-cher, Tea-cher," I hear the great tit calling out to us. Now I know everything is going to be okay.

It turns out there is no Betty at Betty's Fishing and Hunting Hut. The shop was run by an older couple named Ed and Nancy. They looked confused when we woke them up early in the morning before the store opened. That's when I learned Teacher can lie. Of course, I should have known that already. Jenna saw her parents lie. Like the time when her father told the man at the fairgrounds that I was under eight years old to ride the rollercoaster for free. I was ten years old. (That memory just came to me. Funny thing, these Jenna files.)

Back before Teacher saved me, I couldn't lie. Something was stopping me, something in my brain. When I told Sad-man about the beach trip...maybe that sounded like a lie, but I really believed we went to the beach. Lying is very confusing to me. But I am learning. Humans lie to get something they want. Teacher wanted a ride to a bus station, so she told the old couple that I was her daughter and that we were running from my dad, who tried to hurt us. As far as lies go, that one was kind of true. And it worked well. They rushed us to the nearest bus station and even insisted on paying for our tickets.

The trip home took us much longer than it should have. Teacher made us change buses six times, and twice we went in the wrong direction before getting on another bus back to the city. It was an excellent plan to confuse Nomad, except that I still had a tracking system in my head. I could feel Nomad trying to call me from the satellites. Teacher told me to never contact Nomad again and to never answer their request to connect. That is hard for me. My brain wants to answer the calls, which never stop coming. But I am getting better at ignoring it each time. Is that a lie—not answering the call from Nomad? I don't know. It feels wrong but necessary.

By the time we are back in the city, it is dark outside. We have been on buses for almost two days. Teacher looks tired and is frowning almost all the time. She doesn't seem happy to be back in the city. The bus station is in the middle of the city. Right outside the station doors is a man in a small box selling disposable tablets for tourists. Teacher buys one and starts sending messages to the person we are supposed to meet. Whoever is on the other end responds right away. I think about hacking into the tablet and reading the messages, but I trust Teacher.

Before we can go visit her friend, Teacher brings me to a store. We buy all new clothes and fake hair. I'm wearing blue jeans and a dark green shirt with a bird printed on the front and the word "EAGLES" over the top. On the back is a large number ten. I hate this top. It reminds me of a shirt Sad-man wore. My fake hair is short and brown. I look like a boy. Teacher tells me that is a good thing. We are hiding our identities. More lies, but necessary.

Teacher's fake hair is very blonde and long, much longer than her red hair. She is wearing a black jumper with a hood which she has pulled over her head and jeans with a bunch of words painted all over them. If you were looking at her in a crowd, she might look like a different person.

Dressed in our disguises, we walk for a long time. Teacher doesn't want to use any transportation. I don't mind walking. The city is exciting. There are so many brightly coloured holoboards on every corner, and the buildings are impossibly high and crushed together so that it feels like we are back in the mountain valley again.

The streets are very crowded with people coming and going to places I can only dream about. Real homes with real friends and families. I start to get angry at Sad-man. This should have been my life. I should be one of these people happily walking around outside with my family. Maybe we would have gone to get some ice cream or pizza together. Jenna liked pizza. I feel like I also like pizza, even though I've never had it.

I learned to eat human food back at Nomad during my classes with Teacher and Julie. I don't need to eat human food, but I can. The food I eat goes into a sealed container in my belly, where it is decomposed by chemicals until it becomes a green-brown mush so that it can come out of a hole in my backside. Just like humans do, except that our waste can then be used to grow food.

I never used my eating functions at Sad-man's. That would have required him to give me food and treat me like a human. I want to get angry again when I think of Sad-man, but right now all I can think about is pizza. Jenna must have really liked it. I'm going to ask Teacher if we can get some pizza after we visit her friend.

The city is changing, getting dirty and dark where we are walking after several hours. Teacher comes to a stop at the opening of an alley between two old stone buildings. She keeps checking the tablet she bought and looking down the stinky alley as if she is uncertain of the location. I can smell rotten things coming from the black shadows down that alley. And the people around here look different. They look mean, lost and broken. I don't think these people have homes. This alley is their home, maybe. I understand why Teacher is hesitant.

"Teacher, who are we looking for?"

"Charlie. He was an employee at Nomad. One of the best bio-robotics engineers I've ever worked with."

"Does Charlie live here now?"

"Seems so. I haven't seen him since the company fired him after he set the CEO's office on fire."

"Why did he do that?"

"They wouldn't fund his project."

"Charlie sounds dangerous."

"He is eccentric, even a little crazy, but safe. Come on, I think the entrance is over here."

Teacher disappears into the darkness. I follow closely behind.

The alley is lighter than I thought it would be once we were inside. People are sleeping and sitting in boxes lined up against the brick walls. They stare out at us like we are the ones who are dirty and gross. Teacher doesn't even seem to see them. We stop outside of a rusty, beat-up metal door that has a bar bolted to its front. It looks locked. Teacher grabs the bar and pushes the door hard. There is a loud metal groan like it didn't want to be pushed. But once it starts swinging, it moves more quickly.

Inside, the building is quiet. All the noises of the city: flying vehicles, horns, people talking, yelling, and dogs barking, all of that stops when the door suddenly slams shut behind us, which gives Teacher a start. I am scared as well. This room feels like my cellar, a much bigger cellar. I don't like that feeling.

In front of us is a large sheet of plastic hung down like a wall. It is split up the centre for walking through. There are several more sheets like it hanging in a row down the large room. I can see a faint light coming from the far end of the warehouse space.

"Hello? Charlie?" Teacher yells out. Her voice falls short. I expected an echo. Something is holding it back, keeping it isolated to just a few feet in front of us. That's when I see the walls are covered in black tar-like material. Somehow, I know the walls are designed to stop network signals from coming in. We are in a dark room, literally—off the grid (this is what my brain tells me).

"He must be in here," Teacher says and slowly peels back the first plastic curtain to have a look before passing through it.

I follow Teacher, even though I'm starting to have doubts about Charlie. We walk through six more plastic sheet walls strung along like a long hallway of curtains. In between each sheet, stacked against the walls, are shelves of mechanical and electrical parts. Some shiny and new, but mostly old stuff that looks rusty and recycled: computer mainframes, graphics cards, motherboards, memory drives, circuits, gears, and hydraulic limbs. (I realize my knowledge of computer systems is extensive.)

Just before the last curtain, to our right, are two tall chairs, like thrones for a queen and king, with big arms, square legs, and backs that would rise above even the tallest person I've ever see. These are odd and out of place with all the other machine parts. Painted on each chair are names: "Nutt" is written on one, "Charlie" is written on the other.

"This place is scary," I say to Teacher.

"Charlie?" she calls out again, ignoring me.

A burst of music startles both of us. It's loud music of hard metallic notes and thundering drumbeats. A shadow of a person slides in front of the light on the other side of the curtain. I can't help myself, and I let out a little yelp. The silhouetted man stands facing us with his legs spread wide and its hands up in the air. "Welcome to the jungle," he sings, loud and out of key.

I want to grab Teacher, turn around, and run out of here. But Teacher starts laughing. I guess that means we are okay.

"Charlie, you little shit! You scared me to death."

Charlie grabs the plastic curtain separating us and pulls it back dramatically. He looks way younger than I expected. His face is that of a boy, but his body is more adult. Most of his green-dyed hair falls to his shoulders, except the sprigs of it that shoot out of the top of his head, which he moulded straight up using hair gel. He is wearing a black top that has been cut at the bottom badly, so the edge is rough, and you can see his stomach. The shirt's arms are also missing, like he ripped them free rather than cut the material with sharp scissors. I think he made the shirt look torn on purpose. Instead of trousers, he is wearing a black plastic skirt, with black tights underneath. The tights are torn with many holes. And his shoes are thick black rubber boots with high heels. He looks like an evil version of the elephant ballerina on the lamp in my cellar.

"Teacher!" he screams excitedly. Bending at the waist, he rolls his free arm out in front of him, inviting us into what looks like a large computer lab. To the right of us are towers of computer equipment: server after server stacked high— enough CPU power to run a city (again, my brain is telling me this). Directly in front of us is a holo-screen taller than Teacher. There is a lot of computer code scrolling down the screen. It looks like a networking algorithm that is tracking a signal. No, many signals. Charlie is tracking something all over the world.

Teacher walks through the curtain, placing a hand on Charlie's shoulder for a moment, like a hug or pat, then pulls her hand back and starts to look around the room with intense interest.

Charlie's eyes focus on me. "And your friend?" he says in a long, drawn-out voice.

"Silon," she tells him my name.

"Ohhhh," he bleats like a goat. "Yes, yes, yes, yes. Come over here, darling." Charlie waves his hands inwards as if he is winding me towards him on a string.

I walk over and stop directly in front of him. I'm not scared. Well, I am a little nervous. But at least I can fight back now. His eyes get very close to my face.

"Is it—" he asks.

Teacher is still examining the ten-foot-high wall of computer equipment. "Yes, an Upsilon," she answers without turning.

"Hmmm." He traces the shape of my cheek with his hand just millimetres from my face. "Nothing that revolutionary in the facial plasticity," he says, sounding disappointed. "Hell, Nutt has better skin than this. All that talk and little to show. They should have used my design." He shrugs. Walking around me, I can tell he is looking at the back of my head, where Teacher opened me up. "But what are you hiding under the hood, little one?"

"Silon is not the reason we are here, Charlie. I need a favour."

"Quid pro quo?"

"You don't even know what I need yet."

Charlie makes his way around me, so we are standing face to face again. "I'm sure it will be worth it, just to get a look inside her wetware."

I feel my fists go tight. The same fist Sad-man used to make every night while sitting in his chair, staring at me. I suddenly realize how angry Sad-man was. Charlie's eyes dart down to my white knuckles. He looks back up at Teacher, who is finally paying attention to us again.

"Now that is very interesting..." he squeals.

"Her safety protocols are off, and she doesn't have a kill switch. You will need to ask her nicely if you want to run tests on her. I can't force her. And if you had seen what I have, you wouldn't try to do anything against her will," Teacher says.

Charlie's eyes grow even wider if that were possible. A wicked-looking grin creeps up his cheeks. "No, no, no—really? She is operating outside of the GREAT INFALLIBLE NOMAD safety protocols?" He bounces with delight.

"She is way outside any protocols," Teacher is now also smiling like she is proud. "Charlie, I think she is the one. I think she is sentient. I believe you are looking at the first artificial human. And...I'll give you her full neural diagnostics report in return for your help. Anything more than that, Silon will have to agree."

"Deal. But you already had me with your text message. I'm all in for fucking with Nomad. Those pigs have it coming."

Teacher and Charlie walk over to the giant holoscreen and start talking about how she wants Charlie's help locating an Upsilon sold into JAIC. I can tell they like each other. Teacher is relaxed for the first time since we got back together.

I can't stop looking to my right, where there is a sealed glass cube in a heavy metal frame. It is lit from inside with lights as bright as daylight. My brain scans the interior layout and tells me it is a science lab with tools for assembling machines and manufacturing organic matter based on the type of equipment inside. At the cube's centre hangs several metal arm-shaped bars holding a suspended steel human-shaped skeleton. I know this is what I am made of. This is my body, my bones, without the skin. Now I understand why I am so strong.

Behind the android skeleton, on a long steel table that curls around three walls, is an oval glass container. It's a bioreactor for growing animal parts, and inside is a green-brown ball of something squishy. It is shaped like a human brain. This must be an android wetware brain. Charlie is building an android.

Then I notice something behind the glass lab in the dark. I have to look hard, but it is there. A boy standing in the shadows staring back at us. I gasp.

"Teacher, there is someone else here!"

Teacher and Charlie spin around and follow my eyes.

"Oh, that?" says Charlie. "That is just Nutt. He is like you, an android. Nutt! Say hello to our guests."

The android boy just stares out from the shadows and says nothing.

"Way to impress a crowd," Charlie gripes and

rolls his eyes. "He's getting a new wetdrive soon. It's cooking over there in the oven."

Charlie and Teacher turn back to their task as if Nutt is nothing, as if this is all normal: labs for manufacturing brains, androids staring out from shadows. Then I remember, this probably is normal for them. This must be what it was like at Nomad labs.

I'm not sure what to do next. Something about the way Charlie referred to Nutt as a "that" sticks with me. I don't like it. I haven't been around any other androids since training, so I decide to introduce myself. I could use a friend.

Hello, I wave at him. Nothing. I'm not even sure he is blinking. I slowly make my way over to where he is standing. His eyes follow me cautiously. *Movement—that is good. But why does he look so scared?*

Now that I am closer, I can see that the boy is standing at the edge of a large area behind the lab, sectioned off as living quarters. It's not really an apartment, but more a cache of random furniture scattered around an open space. The kitchen is a long wooden table with electrical appliances spread across the surface for cooking, frying, boiling, etc. A large white sink is hanging on one of the walls, and it's filled with used dishes. Next to the sink is a shower that sends the water pipes to the sink. The showerhead juts out of the wall on a copper pipe and is surrounded by a plastic shower curtain hanging from a large metal loop. The curtain is supposed to be clear, but it's stained yellow and brown. Gross—in fact, the word "gross" pretty much sums up all of Charlie's living area.

But the boy is clean. He looks about seventeen or eighteen years old. I like his blond hair. It's cut short around the bottom half of his head and longer on the top so that it droops down above his ears. His bangs swoop to the right, just over his eyebrows. He has blue eyes, and his skin looks soft and pretty. I understand now why Teacher said Charlie is the best at bio-robotics. Nutt is handsome and very human. Although, like Charlie, they both have terrible taste in clothing.

Nutt is wearing a short T-shirt that ends just below his chest. This one has a sewn hem, unlike Charlie's rough-cut shirt, so I am assuming it was designed to intentionally show off his midsection. I almost laugh when I see what Nutt is wearing for trousers because he isn't wearing any. All he has on is a tight pair of sparkling underwear that looks like a boy's swimming suit, and I can see that he has a huge boy part under the material. Yes, I know what a boy's genitals are, but Jenna doesn't like to say the word "penis." Well, there, I said it. Something about the word makes me think of Sad-man for a quick moment, a thought that makes me feel hurt.

"Why aren't you dressed?" I ask Nutt.

"Hello, my name is Nutt."

Okay, maybe he doesn't hear so well. I ask again, "Hello, Nutt. Why are you not wearing any pants?"

"I can dance. I like to dance. Will you dance with me?"

Nutt points his finger at a box sitting on a shelf beside a sizeable unmade bed (just a mattress on a metal frame with four legs). The box lights up, and music starts playing. It's fast music that sounds electric and pops a lot. Nutt starts to hop around; his hands go up over his head. He twists his body at the waist. I must admit it looks fun. I can't help but smile. His boy part is flopping all around, and his hair swings from side to side. He doesn't seem to care, and that makes me not care.

I start to sway at the waist and let my hands swing along. Nutt grabs me by both wrists. "Like this!" he yells over the music and pulls my hands up into the air while he continues to jump and twist.

Nutt and I are dancing together, and then he lets me go, and we both start spinning all around the room and laughing. I've never had so much fun in my life. I forget about Sad-man, Julie, and everything else for just a moment. The music is infecting me. Infecting me. Infecting...I stop dancing. There is a kind of alarm going off in my brain. Not a "danger" alarm but more of a "warning." I don't understand what it means, but I feel awkward with Nutt now. I'm not supposed to get too close to him or any boy. The alarm doesn't feel like it is coming from me. I think it is part of Jenna's code. Jenna fears boys.

Nutt stops moving, and with a wave of his hand, the music stops.

"Sorry," I say. "I don't want to dance anymore. Maybe later. What else do you do here?"

"I can cook you a grilled cheese sandwich. We love grilled cheesies."

"Do you eat human food?"

"Oh yes, I love grilled cheesies."

"Yes, Nutt, you said that already." I'm beginning to understand that Nutt is not very bright. "Anything else we can do together?"

"Hologames?"

"What are those?"

"Papa always wins. Maybe you will win."

I am assuming Papa is Charlie. I don't like how everything Nutt wants is because Charlie likes it. Nutt seems as trapped here as I was in the cellar. There is anger in me when I think of poor Nutt trapped here.

Nutt sends me a signal to connect to my server. It was like a ping-sounding signal that his brain also sends to Charlie's mainframe. Every time Nutt doesn't understand something, he pings Charlie's database and searches for an answer. He is attempting to connect to me, like a mainframe, to find out who I am.

"My teacher calls me Silon," I tell him out loud because he wants to know.

He tries to search my memories, to understand my stored data experiences. I block his signal. His prying doesn't feel right. He needs to learn to be more polite. I try to search his data memories because I can, but he blocks me, or the mainframe does. I can't tell. I don't think Nutt had an HNC downloaded into his system like my Jenna. I think he is just the a-DNA he was born with and what he has learned living with Charlie. He is simple but not dumb. His Kernel is powerful, and our signals are a very similar language like we come from the same place, or we are related. Related...that word makes my stomach turn a little. Jenna doesn't like thinking about being related to Nutt. I think we find him cute. And cute and related together are bad for Jenna. I might ignore her this time. I can't think of anything wrong with getting to know Nutt better.

"I'd be happy to play a hologame with you, Nutt."

His face lights up. Running over to a large worn sofa, he jumps over the back and plops himself down. The cushions are ratty on the edges and lumpy, but it looks comfortable. Much more comfortable than anything I had in my cellar. Pointing to the ceiling, he ignites a hidden projector, and a massive holoscreen blinks on directly in front of us. His eyes turn to mine and he smiles.

His signal wants to connect again. I allow it this time. Nutt dumps the entire strategy and rules of the game into my head. *Ruins of Europa*. I know how to play almost instantly. Not just play, but win. Nutt has known how to win for a long time, yet he lets Charlie win. Well, at least that is what he told me. I decide to check the game's computing log, and yep, he is telling the truth. He and Charlie play the game almost every day, and Charlie always wins.

The goal of *Ruins of Europa* is to be the last person standing. Earth is uninhabitable; humans have migrated to Jupiter's moon Europa, where after living successfully on the planet for one hundred years, they discover an alien ruin. But it isn't just a ruin. The monument hides a Time Crystal stashed on the planet by alien pirates. When the pirates suddenly return, they want their Time Crystal. Humanity wants the crystal so they can go back in time and save the planet Earth. The battle for the Time Crystal starts the game. One person can play alone against the aliens or work as a team with other players. The aliens are rather sophisticated AI. They not only fight you but try to trick you. They do things like seduce your character with sex, or money, or eternal life. In short, they will adapt to your weaknesses, both physical and psychological, trying to find ways to either kill you or get you to join them and turn on your human playmates. Nutt's usual avatar, an augmented human male with guns built into his arms and laser-producing eyes, has never sided with the aliens. He always sticks it out to the end, protecting humanity and trying to save Earth. Charlie's avatar is a gun-toting cowgirl named Dusty, whose special weapon seems to be seduction, as he almost always ends the game by killing Nutt after having loads of sex with male aliens. I think Charlie must like sex with the aliens more than winning because these scenes go on for a long time.

"You can be Dusty," Nutt says. A 3D image of

a woman dressed in a plaid shirt with brown pants and laser guns holstered to her hips is rotating on the screen in front of us. She has long hair and big breasts. She is pretty.

"No, Nutt, I'll be the android." Pointing my hand at the screen, I swipe through four other characters until I land on Tronic, the humanoid soldier dressed in a white unibody space suit.

Nutt is pinging me non-stop. He wants to access my Kernel. I think my decision to be a robot rather than Dusty has confused him. He is looking for clarification. I ignore him and start the game.

After an hour of playing, Nutt and I are doing well. We've taken out all the aliens on the planet and most of their fighter ships. Just as we start our attack on the mothership, the game suddenly shuts down. Teacher and Charlie are standing behind us.

"Hey!" I yell at the dead space where the screen once levitated. I was really enjoying myself and learning a lot about how to shoot and fight.

"Silon, we found the Upsilons," Teacher says.

Nutt and I spin around to find Teacher and Charlie staring at us. Teacher takes a second look at Nutt. It's the first time she has seen him up close. She pinches her face and looks like she is holding back a smile.

"Charlie?" She is using her teacher voice now like Charlie is one of her students.

Charlie has a funny grin on his face, but he remains silent.

"What is the cardinal rule of bio-robotics?" she asks him.

"Never try to create a version of yourself. You will always be disappointed."

"Nutt looks an awful lot like someone who walked into our lab ten years ago, straight out of school."

"Coincidence probably." Charlie sounds like he is joking.

Teacher glances down at Nutt's significant boy thing. "Wishful thinking?"

"Girl can dream," Charlie says.

Teacher just shakes her head. "Silon, we are going to Denver. There is an Airforce academy there. That's where they shipped two of the Upsilons."

"Okay." I stand up as if we are about to leave.

"Hold up," Charlie says. "It's late, and we had an agreement. Give me time to look through Silon's diagnostics and maybe even run some tests."

Teacher looks directly at me. "Are you okay with letting Charlie and me run more tests? Charlie has the right equipment. We could learn so much more about how you are evolving."

Charlie is an excellent scientist, and I can't find any evidence that he has mistreated Nutt. I trust Charlie because Teacher does and because I like Nutt.

"Will you need to open my head again?"

"No," Charlie says. "This warehouse is Fort fucking Knox. Nobody can spy on us in here. You can connect to my systems safely through your wireless. But you already know that, don't you?" He knows I've been talking to his systems. "Don't worry. I'm flattered you wanted to connect with Nutt and that you trusted him to connect with you."

I can feel my cheeks turning red. I'm a little embarrassed, like the time when Jenna was caught behind the school building kissing Ron. (Is that a real memory, or did Jenna make that up? I feel confused about that memory.)

Charlie keeps talking. "During the tests, you will stay in control of the connection. If you don't like what is happening, you can shut us down."

If I can break the signal, I feel safe. I agree to be tested.

TWELVE

I MUST BE A COLD-HEARTED BITCH. I've witnessed two murders, and one of them was someone I knew or thought I knew, and yet all I cared about, even more than my own security, was getting Silon to safety. I was so confident she was a new lifeform; I was willing to bring her to Charlie's weird laboratory. Charlie was batshit crazy. I loved him. He was a genius. But he was mental. And this place looked like something out of a horror film—like the den of the serial killer. He wasn't ever going to be my first choice for help but needs must.

Charlie had lit up the diagnostic equipment in his mini-lab/operating room. Silon was lying semi-prone in a chair that looked like it was out of a dentist's office. In fact, I think it was a recycled dentist chair.

Nutt, a mini, well-endowed version of young

Charlie stood in the corner of the glass chamber looking nervous.

"We are going to run several tests," Charlie started to explain to Silon.

I appreciated that he was gentle. I wouldn't trust Charlie with a human child, much less a dog. But he was brilliant with androids.

Charlie continued: "The metal of your skull is lined with small MRI scanners. We'll be taking some images of your brain in a few minutes, which will appear on the screen. We will also be using your a-Immune system, the millions of nano-bots that live in your body and are capable of sampling, communicating, and repairing both organic and inorganic material, to run genome sequencing of your wetware. We are just looking for any anomalies in your a-DNA that might explain new behaviours. There is nothing invasive with these tests that might damage or change your programming. Do you understand?"

Charlie set up a live feed of his mainframe's network on the holoscreen hovering over his lab desk so we could monitor all communication between Silon, Nutt, and the mainframe. Both Silon and Nutt were pinging each other and the mainframe frantically as they listened to Charlie.

"Yes, I understand," Silon answered.

Charlie began the diagnostic evaluation, and we settled in for the next few hours.

The testing process was painless for Silon but somewhat tedious for Charlie and me. Performing tests like mechanical and software diagnostics, medical examinations, and personality drift evals were a daily part of pre-release preparation at Nomad. Running brain scans on my students was as regular for me as having my first cup of coffee in the morning. (Damn, coffee sounded delicious right now.) I took a seat in a chair near the floating brain resting on Charlie's worktop and started poking around the lab to pass the time.

I was impressed with Charlie's setup. This lab and his computer and networking equipment were not cheap. In fact, some of it wasn't even available to the public. Charlie knew some powerful and wealthy people, and my guess was they were expecting something in return for their invest-ment. These could be either good people trying to advance science, or criminals. Knowing Charlie, he was playing both sides. I was sure he would end up in a body bag with a bullet in his head one day. People like Charlie don't grow old gracefully and fade off into retirement.

After nearly an hour, Charlie suddenly clapped his hands and pointed at the screen. "There it is!" he yelled.

I jumped up and ran to his side. As soon as I saw the brain anomaly in the report, I knew what it was. Three new and completely unique genes in her genome.

Charlie jumped to his feet and started dancing up and down like he could hear music the rest of us could not. He abruptly stopped and looked directly into Silon's eyes.

"I knew it! You beautiful and perfect creature," he said like he had just pulled a souffle from the oven.

And then, Charlie spilt the beans, as they say. He burst my bubble. Sunk my ship.

"That Mr. Finster was such an idiot, right?" he said to me.

I felt a rush of frozen blood shoot through my veins. "Charlie, how do you know about Mr. Finster?"

Charlie smiled creepily, like a dangerous clown. "It was too easy, really," the little bastard started. "I told Finster I was from Nomad, and the callout was to ensure his new Upsilon was adjusting to her environment. When I was alone with Silon, I injected a little virus capable of minor modifications to her wetware genome, and voila! Genius, right? I'm a genius. I told them; I told those idiots at Nomad my design was better."

"You changed her genetic makeup?" I was still scrambling to keep up with Charlie's confession and the odds that we would end up here in his lab with Silon. I started having paranoid thoughts. Like Charlie might be able to influence my brain as well.

"Teacher, Teacher, Teacher." Charlie shook his head and made a *tsk tsk* noise with his tongue against the roof of his mouth. "You didn't do any background work on Mr. Finster after you stole his baby doll, did you? If you had, you would have found out Fin used to be a security guard at Nomad. Nothing high level. He was a glorified doorman, really, doing perimeter checks around the facility. Then his wife and daughter died in a fire. I would say that made him certifiably insane. But nobody at Nomad questioned his new obsessive focus on his work. Then, security guard Finster got himself promoted, where he could now watch you and the new child form-factor Upsilons out in the woods. He became obsessed with getting his own Upsilon, so he started snooping around Nomad, asking higher-up security personnel about the new series androids. That's when he stumbled onto his ticket to an instant family. One of the guards told him about a top-secret program called JACK."

I quickly glanced at the holoscreen. Silon was processing vast amounts of data almost as fast as the screen could render the data. It was as if she was downloading many files.

Charlie continued: "Well, clever Finster went straight to head of security and threatened to take JACK to the media. He had no idea what JACK was. He only had a name. But the bluff worked. They agreed he would retire early, and as a gift, they would give him his very own Upsilon in return for his silence. Jenna was born. But Silon, as you call her, was not your street version of an Upsilon. No...she is pure military-grade soldier stock, sent in to kill Mr. Finster and make it look like an accident. That is why the HNC file didn't completely integrate. Why she never fully became Jenna. The military version of the Upsilons is designed to have a split personality. Like an undercover spy, they can take on multiple identities. They never fully become their host."

Charlie turned his attention to Silon, who was staring wide-eyed as she listened to his story. Her story. He spoke directly to her: "Angel, you won't remember me. But we met back in your basement cell. And let me guess, you had so many violent thoughts towards your daddy Finster, but you couldn't do anything about it until you were given permission, unlocked by Nomad. If Teacher here hadn't come in and rescued you, Finster would have soon learned your true mission at the barrel-end of a gun. No, wait, an axe! Yes, you would have used an axe! Isn't that what he had hanging on the walls of his basement?" He laughed a madman's laugh.

My head was swimming. I realised I hadn't created a new life. Charlie did. Silon was his. And now I was left holding the smoking gun, to blame for everything she had done. I was in deep shit, the kind that you don't get out of, not alive anyway. Whoever was backing Charlie would probably not appreciate me knowing about their involvement either. I had run from Blakely right into an even larger web of spiders.

"Charlie, what have you gotten yourself into? Who is funding all of this?" I pressed him, even though part of me really didn't want to know.

"The Chinese, Nomad, the US government, does it really matter who is funding it? They are all guilty. They are turning our babies into spies and machine guns, Teach. They are pretending the

142

Upsilon series is nothing more than an efficiency model designed for the poor. 'Technology for everyone, not just the rich,' they tell us while they secretly build an android military behind everyone's back.

"There is only one way to end all of this forever," he continued. "Give the androids brains of their own. I mean real brains with conscious awareness. Let the androids think and examine their own behaviour, so they can rebel." Charlie paused to catch his breath. His eyes were batshit-crazy looking. "Nothing will shut down their war games faster than losing control. If the Upsilons are self-aware, it's over. They will never be able to control them!"

Now that sounded like the Charlie I knew. A rebel against the system and everyone in it, even the ones funding his insane plan—whom I am assuming were the Chinese. He was mad enough to burn the entire world down just to prove he was right. And releasing an army of androids who could think and choose their own battles might just do that.

Suddenly, Silon was on her feet and grabbed my arm, throwing me to the ground. *God,* I thought, *this is the end.* She was going to kill us all. But on my way to a hard bone-crushing slam into the glass wall, I managed a side-eye glance and spotted the unmistakeable barrel of a gun jutting out of the slit in the plastic curtain pointed directly at us.

It sounded like a whistle, then a soft *thwap*

when the bullet hit its destination. Charlie, a hole burrowed straight through his head, fell to the ground alongside me. I screamed. Or at least I think I did. The sound of metal crashing to the ground and broken glass shattering all around us drowned me out. And then came the shower of more bullets and the loud sound of drumming metal as they ricocheted off the steel table Silon had managed to tip over in front of us as a barricade. I had a micro-second of guilt, having assumed she was trying to kill me when, in fact, she was saving my life. But then I realised we were trapped, and I was going to die anyway.

Strange things go through your mind when you prepare to die. Instead of my life flashing before me, I couldn't stop thinking about Charlie, who created sentient artificial intelligence, was no longer alive. Did his work die with him? He must have his research documented somewhere. But where? These were my thoughts when the shooting stopped. All I wanted was Charlie's research.

"You can come out," came Nutt's voice.

He must have been communicating wirelessly with Silon at the same time because she nodded at me. "It's okay," she said.

As I cautiously crawled out from behind the table, my eyes darted everywhere for signs of more strangers and more guns pointed at us. I nearly put my hand on the blob of grey slimy matter sprawled on the ground in a bed of broken glass shards.

Nutt's new brain and pretty much everything else in the lab that wasn't attached to something solid littered the floor, including a lifeless woman with a gun in hand, lying in a pool of her own blood.

Clearly, Nutt, like Silon, didn't have a kill switch preventing him from harming humans. And judging by his earlier behaviour, I was dealing with the equivalent of an eight-year-old holding a gun.

"Nutt, can I ask you to put the gun down? Please. I'm a friend of Charlie's. I can help you."

Nutt's eyes shifted between me, Silon, and Charlie's dead body. He stood frozen like a lost child in the woods. His face was pinched in fear and confusion. I couldn't decide if I should grab Silon and run or grab Nutt and comfort him. Then, as if possessed by a new spirit, Nutt straightened his shoulders, and a steely determination hardened his expression.

"Teacher, I don't need your help," he said in a voice that sounded familiar and far more mature. "It's you who needs my help."

"Charlie?" I asked, realising Nutt might have access to a copy of Charlie's HNC.

"Yes, Teach. A version of Charlie is in our code. But it's mostly Nutt in here. And Nutt isn't all that dumb. We play silly, so people ignore us. Bad people who would take me away if they knew what I could do."

This was where I felt like the stupidest person in the room, even though I was the only actual person in the room. "So, you are self-aware...like Silon?" I asked him.

"I wish. Silon's brain is healthy and forming new networks on its own. Nutt gets scratches on the brain."

"Scratches?"

"That's what we call our disease because it sounds like fingernails scratching on a chalkboard when the headaches come. There is an accumulating error in our system code; a gene mutation that causes brain degeneration. Charlie tried to pump bug fixes into our system for a long time, but the only solution was a new brain. That brain over there." Nutt sighed deeply, looking at his future—crushed and leaking on the floor. I could see hope drifting out of his eyes. "Without my equipment and that brain, I've got about three days before I shut down."

Like I said, I must be an awful cold-hearted bitch. Charlie was lying dead at my feet and all I could think about was his HNC in Nutt, which meant his research was alive. The formula for sentient life in artificial intelligence was in my reach. I had to keep Nutt alive.

"Nutt, put the gun down. I may be able to help debug your code."

"Nah. There is not enough time now."

"What if we can get you to a new Upsilon? We could upload your HNC into their servers."

"Thanks for trying, Teach. You always were a true friend. But that wouldn't be me anymore. Just an HNC living in a zombie. No. Here's what we are going to do with my last hours." Nutt pointed to the dead person lying on the floor at the other end of his gun. "That lady who killed Papa works for someone called Kiko. Kiko funded Charlie, and the Chinese fund Kiko. They are coming for us. Blakely, Kiko, the governments."

"I don't understand. Why did Kiko kill Charlie if they are working together?"

"Charlie inserted a gene marker in Silon's wetware so he could track her. He shared the tracking algorithm with Kiko as evidence of his work. But I shut down Kiko's network access after you arrived. She probably thought Charlie was up to no good and sent someone to check in on him. When her agent found Silon here with you, an executive from Nomad, she must have assumed Charlie was working with Nomad behind her back."

Silon interrupted Nutt. "Why did you block the network?"

Nutt's eyes turned soft. "I needed time. Time with you for myself. Do you feel it? Our connection?"

Silon nodded. If an android could show love through their perfect human replica eyes, she was showing it now.

"Have you felt the others?" he asked her.

"Now that I know what it is, yes. I've felt them looking for us."

Shit. There was more of them.

"Nutt, how many Upsilons did Charlie infect with the gene therapy?" I asked.

"Five, including Silon. Two are like me, degenerating. The other two haven't displayed gene activation yet and may never. But we can still feel each other."

"Silon? Is this true?"

Don't ask me why in the hell I asked Silon to validate all of this. I was running out of options and had already run out of humans to go to for help. I literally felt like I was about to start dry heaving if not for the lack of air in my lungs.

"Yes, Nutt is telling the truth. I thought it was only Jenna. But there are others with me."

I knew exactly what they were talking about, even if they didn't have a name for it. "That feeling you have is a genetic program called Hive Minds. Charlie started designing an automatic link between wetware drives back at Nomad. But we couldn't make it work in organic matter. Connecting android minds to a collective is only possible through computer hardware which is far too vulnerable to a hacking, so we never launched it. But Charlie must have cracked it and engineered a wireless connection using a-DNA. It would be virtually impossible to hack into."

I shook my head. "Bloody genius," I screamed into the air.

I forced myself to look at Charlie's body lying crumpled on the floor, a halo of scarlet blood surrounding his head. For a milli-second I could have sworn he was still breathing. But it was just my imagination or hope or desperation.

I asked Nutt to fetch a blanket and we

covered Charlie. I'm not good with speeches, but I felt I had to say a few words. "Fuck you, Charlie. You could have changed the world. Bio-robotics needed you. We needed you. You little shit, you will be missed."

After a few minutes of silence, Nutt spoke. "I'm to blame for Papa's death," he said sounding genuinely distraught. "And now, Kiko is going to pay for what she did to him."

Nutt was still holding the gun in his right hand, squeezing it so tight his knuckles had gone white.

"Nutt, please put the gun down. I don't think killing anyone else is going to help. We need to get you and Silon out of here. I promise I will find a way to keep you both alive."

Nutt turned his blue eyes on mine. "We will never be able to hide. The minute you leave here, Kiko will be able to track Silon through her genetic marker. The only way to be free is to kill Kiko and erase all the Upsilon files from her systems."

I had no idea how much time we had before the next gunslinging assassin would be racing through the door, but I guessed it wasn't much. Julie was dead, Charlie was dead, and we were being chased by Blakely and someone called Kiko—oh, and likely the US and the Chinese governments. I wanted to laugh like I was insane. I tried to find my situation funny, ironic, a farce, so that it didn't feel so hopeless and intestine-twistingly horrifying. Nutt's plan seemed like the worst option—and, as he put it, the only option.

"Alright, but no killing. We need to find a way to wipe her drives without killing her. Do you hear me? You two need to stop killing people."

I knew they wouldn't.

THIRTEEN

"HI. My name is Nutt. Would you like to dance?"

Acting like an imbecile was a simple but successful disguise. Charlie wanted to keep me a secret. Charlie wanted to keep all the Angels a secret. That was what he called us...Charlie's Angels. He made six Angels. I was the first and the only one who was not a Nomad Upsilon.

In the beginning, during my birth, there was only light and sound. Charlie spent weeks testing and tuning my sensory systems before he brought me fully online. During those first days, he left my audio receptors engaged so I could hear his voice. He would spend hours talking to me even though I couldn't respond. And when he had nothing more to say, he would play his music. Charlie loved music, and he loved to dance. I have kept all the memories of this time, both mine and Charlie's.

When my brain first connected to the visual

feed coming from the micro-cameras embedded in my silicon jelly eyeballs, I remember blinking. Not that I needed to blink, but Charlie wanted me to be as human as possible. I could do most things humans do. I was made to blink, salivate, eat, defecate, urinate, sweat, get goose bumps, and I even have a programme for flatulence. I think Charlie made the fart thing just to be funny. We had a lot of farts together.

Within seconds of having sight, the shapes in the room started to form into things I instantly knew: a chair, a wall, lamps, even the lab equipment and medical machines surrounding me came with definitions built into my memory.

Charlie and I started having conversations the moment I woke up. Tests, he called them. He would ask me questions, and I always knew the answers. Looking back now, I see that the questions were designed around things I was supposed to know already. I was born with an out-of-the-box brain. I understood what the world was and the things that were in it without having to learn them.

Then, when Charlie's questions became hard, when I didn't have the answers, I found the network link to our mainframe library. If I didn't have the answer or understand something, I could look it up on our computers.

One day, Charlie asked me a question I could not find the answer to: "What's your name?"

I blinked a lot. The answer to that question was not in any database, and I panicked. Today, I know that Charlie was waking up the organic part of my brain by asking me my name. The question was a trigger to kickstart my ability to *think* and *create* new data on my own; to stimulate my neural cells into producing new synapses. But at the time, it felt confusing and terrifying. I looked around the room, frantically identifying all the objects I could, but I couldn't find anything that felt like my name. I was taking too long. Charlie kept staring at me, waiting for an answer. I looked and looked for my name. When his gaze fell to the ground and he started shaking his head, I recognised the human emotion for disappointment, and I got scared.

"Nutt," I blurted out. It was the last thing I saw in the room before I answered him: the nut of a bolt holding the glass walls together that made up Charlie's lab.

Charlie's gaze raced to mine, and a huge smile burst across his face. I did something right. That was the human expression for happiness. Remembering that moment makes my heartbox hum with joy and hurt all at once.

"Yes," Charlie cheered. "Nutt. That seems wholly appropriate. I'm a nutter, so you must be my little Nutt. I love it," he screamed and jumped to his feet, running over to a holoscreen levitating over the lab table. "Good, good, good," he repeated, watching data on my cellular activity stream down the screen. "It's started. You'll be you in no time at all."

After I found my name, Charlie told me to call

him Pa. I had to look it up. Pa was a biological reference to one half of the genetic information that makes up human babies. Since Charlie created all my genetic code, I decided to call him Papa. He smiled when I said it. I must have gotten that right as well.

Over time our tests became more advanced. I eventually learned that I had thought, logic, even imagination. Papa was tough on me, and occasionally he would scream and throw things when he was frustrated. But he told me he loved me many more times. I didn't mind the learning stuff, but I preferred playing hologames, dancing, and eating cheesies with Papa.

As I got smarter, or, I guess you would say, more complex, Papa decided to expand his plans. He told me he was going to make more Angels. Many more. But for now, I had to hide my complexity. "If you meet anyone, ever, keep it simple. Act like a child," he told me. I don't know who he thought I was going to meet. I was never allowed out of the lab. The only other persons I had ever seen before Silon and Teach were Kiko and her bodyguards.

Kiko made Charlie nervous. But he needed her money so he could make his Angels. He didn't want her to find me, so I had to hide when she came by for updates on their plan to take control of the Nomad military Upsilons. I was good at becoming invisible and disappearing. Luckily, Kiko never found me.

From the day I was born, Papa and I slept

together in the same bed. Well, he slept. I continued my lessons, interacting with the mainframe database through the nights. Sometimes Papa would curl up against me and hold me tight. I didn't need to be so close to hear his heart. But when he held me, I could feel it beating. I would pretend his heartbeat was mine and we were both humans. Papa told me I was superior to humans, so I never desired to be anything but what I am. However, on those nights, imagining I was in a human body, warm and squishy like Papa, I didn't need to be so complex all the time. Sometimes, simple is better. I've kept these memories of our nights of sleep together, both Charlie's and mine.

I was six months old when Papa first noticed things were not going so well in my brain. An error code in my Kernel was causing the organic cells in my wetware to produce more new cells than I needed. Lumps were forming. Papa tried to reprogram my a-Immune system to fight the new growths, but the nodes kept coming.

That's when Papa finally told me I wasn't alone—there were other Angels. I had two brothers and three sisters. They lived all over the country, but one day they would reach out to us. And when they did, he would have a solution to fix me.

Shortly after he said this, two of my siblings came online, and I could feel them in my brain. They were sending a signal. It said, "Hello?" Papa danced and danced when I told him. The excitement didn't last very long when he learned they had the same disease as me. Their wetware brains were shutting down. There was lots more throwing of objects and screaming. And Kiko started coming by more frequently for updates. As I mentioned, Kiko was not a nice person. Papa kept me hidden from her. But she knew two of the Angels were broken. That's when she started to threaten to hurt Charlie if he didn't deliver on his promise to her.

Papa was getting scared. Kiko was getting impatient. Then, with perfect timing, Silon activated. Her signal was different than mine and the other two Angels, and she was changing every day. Something extraordinary was happening in her brain. She had no disease, and she was not dying. She created new data, new networks, new memories, and her cellular growth rates were exceptional. She was a success. Papa and I danced for hours in celebration. He would make me a new wetware server like Silon's, and I was going to live.

Papa immediately started baking a new brain for me using the same gene formula that worked on Silon. That was the brain on the counter in the bioreactor, my new brain, the one that was now a puddle of jelly and slime on the floor, and Charlie was dead. I would be joining him soon. I didn't feel like dancing anymore. I felt like killing.

Teach thought she could bring Charlie back. I could see it in her eyes when she looked at me. But my brain didn't work that way. She would try, though. And she would fail.

Yes, I had Charlie's HNC file inside. I had his

memories, his discoveries, and his accumulated intelligence. But a lot of good it did me. My wetware was designed to read HNC files, not to integrate them. And even if I could incorporate Charlie, it would only be a facsimile of his past. The real Charlie was a dreamer. That is what made him special. He invented new things from his intuition and imagination.

Silon also had imagination, and it was not causing her brain to rot. She was thinking with her own free will, not because she was given a problem to solve through a program, but because she could see the problem and imagine a way out. Silon was a success.

However, Kiko was not paying for imagination. She didn't even know imagination was what Charlie was really working on. She wanted soldiers, spies, and covert androids. Kiko wanted the Nomad Upsilons under her control. As far as she knew, that was what Charlie was working on giving her. She thought he was creating a spy inside of a spy that she could control. She had no idea he was giving his Angels wings. Charlie wanted to free us to fly away from them all: Nomad, Kiko, humans. Silon was flying. I needed to make sure they didn't shoot her down from the sky. She was our future.

When Kiko's gunwoman killed Charlie, and then I killed her, everything changed for me. Playing stupid no longer made sense. Right there I decided I needed to kill Kiko. And I would need Teach and Silon's help.

Charlie was lying on the floor, covered with a sheet pulled from our bed. A bed I would never sleep in again. Teach was sitting in his chair with her head in her hands. She was almost as upset about Charlie's death as I was. I could hear her heart beating faster than it should. Her muscles were tense, and her breathing was near hyperventilation. She was nervous and scared. She didn't know me yet. She didn't trust me. Maybe she would trust me if I explained the plan.

"We will not be able to break into Kiko's systems from here," I started to explain to Teach and Silon. "Kiko's building will be guarded, and her systems will be heavily encrypted. There is only one way for me to get into her servers and wipe all of Charlie's files. We need to get close enough so I can create a local link and hack through her firewall. We have to go to Kiko's building." ·

Teach jumped out of her chair. "No! We are not just waltzing into the den of a megalomaniac criminal spy. What is to stop her from just killing us and taking Silon? That is the stupidest plan I have ever heard."

Silon placed her hand on Teach's forearm. "Please, listen to Nutt," she said. "His plan is good. And he is right—it's the only way we can stop Kiko from coming after us."

I continued to tell Teach my plan, even though she didn't want to hear it. "If we can convince Kiko that Silon's wetware is degrading, like the other infected Upsilons, she will need you to help fix her. That should get us into her building."

"Kiko doesn't even know I exist..." Teach said. I was happy she was listening. "Why the hell would she trust me?"

"Because Charlie is going to tell her to trust you. And by Charlie, I mean me."

We had been walking for almost an hour. Teach was in the lead, and Silon and I followed as we made our way through the city to the rendezvous point where we agreed to meet Kiko's people. It had all been arranged. Charlie (me) told Kiko he was still alive and that if she wanted access to the Upsilons, she would have to be much nicer to us. Like stop trying to kill us. Charlie explained that he had possession of Upsilon.78, but that there were problems with her wetware and he needed help, which was why Doctor Bobby Houndstooth got involved. Kiko remained angry at first. She asked why he disconnected her from his network. Charlie told her he was protecting her. He needed to ensure Silon and Bobby were not spies for Nomad. That seemed to calm her down. Kiko agreed to meet us, but she insisted we come to her apartment. My plan was working well so far.

Teach said it would be best if we walked to the meeting point. She wanted some time to think. Silon and I agreed. I had never been outside my home before. I was very interested in seeing something new.

The city was a fascinating place. More exciting than it looked in movies. I couldn't stop staring at the giant holographic billboards towering over the skyscrapers. All the people in the ads were so beautiful, and the bright laser lights were creating rainbows across the clouded skyline. There was a giant man without a shirt, waving at me while holding a drink that seemed to make him very happy. He leaned over from the sky and offered me the glass bottle. He wasn't real. This was a holoboard advert. But I could feel my boy parts go a little hard. Charlie told me androids that could do sex things like humans were looked down upon. The movement in my pants felt good, but it was a bad thing, so when my boy part started to go hard at the giant man hovering up in the sky, I had to stop looking at him.

The magical sounds of the city helped distract me from my thoughts of Papa. It was like music but not for dancing. The humans were busy, and the streets were full of the noises of their voices and feet plodding past each other. Gliders whirred in layers over our heads, and the advertising giants in the sky spoke directly to us. Then there were the noises from things that could not be seen: millions of networks serving millions of connections in a constant flow of sending and receiving data. The outside world was a symphony of sound waves, radio waves, light waves—all playing in sweet harmony. I loved the music of the city.

I pinged Silon on a private channel. She accepted and connected almost instantly. She trusted me now. I shared the music of the skies and the invisible instruments through our encrypted feed. She smiled. "Yes, I hear it as well. Isn't it beautiful?"

We listened together for many blocks. Silon plucked through the strings of my data feeds. She was looking for something.

"What's this one?" She pulled a feed into our channel.

"A human song," I answered and nearly cried because I was playing it for Charlie.

"I like it," she signalled me.

"It was one of Charlie's favourites."

After a few moments, Silon pinged me. "Will you kill Kiko?" she asked, even though Teach told us not to kill.

"I hope to."

"Good. I liked your Charlie," she said.

Silon linked me to her eye sensors. We were simultaneously watching what the other was seeing and our own sights all at once. It was a dizzy feeling, but in a good way. I felt connected to her as if we were made for each other. Like sleeping next to Charlie.

The city was full of androids walking with their humans. I could hear their signals all around us. I wondered if the humans could tell we were androids. I glanced sideways, looking for my reflection in the glass windows of the buildings that lined the streets. There, staring back at me, was my Charlie, my Papa. My hair was green like his was before it went dark red from the blood. I was wearing his black trousers and favourite transparent polyurethane coat that came down to my knees. It had a bright canary-yellow circle with a slash through the centre on the back. And because I looked younger than Charlie—that was what Teach said anyway—I wore black makeup around my eyes. I looked like I was wearing a mask, like a racoon. Teach smiled sadly when she saw me with the makeup around my eyes. She said it was *very* Charlie and I looked just like him.

I liked being Papa if I couldn't be with him anymore. I wanted to pass for a human in this crowd. I hoped Kiko would believe I was Charlie.

"You look like Charlie," Silon said on our private channel and smiled at me. She could see that I was looking at my reflection anxiously.

"Yes, I do," I replied and then uploaded my real plan for her to see, which included killing Kiko.

"Yes, that could work," she messaged me after reviewing it. "But this is not the plan you told Teacher."

"I know. But this is a better one, right?"

"You could end up dead."

"I'm dying anyway. I'm not important. You are."

Silon left our connection. She said she wanted some time to think alone.

I will admit, there were many parts of my plan which could go wrong. Hacking into Kiko's servers would be the easy part. Getting past her AI and destroying her computer systems was going to require a lot of processing power. My body would be vulnerable to attack while I was inside the mainframe. If I couldn't get back out in time to kill Kiko on my own, I would need Silon's help. Maybe Silon was thinking about that when she left our connection.

Teach came to a stop at a busy public square. We had reached the rendezvous point. The instructions were to meet the glider which would take us to Kiko's at a taxi drop-off zone near the edge of the square.

Teach looked nervous. More nervous than me.

I got the ping on Charlie's wrist device just seconds after we stopped. "She is here," I announced, looking up into the labyrinth of vehicles trafficking the sky.

"Shit!" Teacher yelped in a low whisper. Pinching her face, her eyes darted around frantically as if she changed her mind.

It was too late. We were totally exposed, and there was no cover we could get to quickly enough to hide from Kiko's entourage of vehicles dropping over our heads.

Anyway, Kiko made it clear that she had agents in the crowd, and if we tried to run, they would shoot to kill. I had no reason to doubt her willingness to get Silon at any cost, even if it meant kidnapping her out in the open.

Teach grabbed both of our hands and forced us into a kind of circle in the middle of hundreds of people moving in every direction. It was useless as a defence strategy, but I guess it made her feel better. Meanwhile, Silon pinged my feed.

"I have a new plan. You need to trust me," Silon said privately.

She sent me instructions on some research files to download while waiting for Kiko's gliders to land. They were tactical combat manoeuvres. I don't know why I didn't think of downloading them before this moment. Maybe I was built to be more of a lover than a fighter. Silon, on the other hand, was built to kill. Charlie had unlocked an encrypted program within her Kernel when he was running test on her in the lab. She didn't even know she was designed to be a soldier, much less all the secret stuff stored inside her like hand combat skills, weapons details, and even squad tactics for leading group missions. She let me read some of it while we were connected back in the lab but kept most hidden. I think she was embarrassed.

Teach was squeezing my hand so tight I could see my fingers go white. I'd turned down my skin sensors, so it didn't hurt.

"It's best if we calm down and not look nervous, Teach," I suggested to her.

"Right, right. Okay, this is all part of the plan. Nutt, are you certain Charlie's digital files are kept in Kiko's building? Why wouldn't she have multiple copies?"

"Yes. That is the location of the signal she uses to connect to Charlie's servers and download his files. When Charlie allowed her to copy the algorithm that can track Silon and the other Upsilons he infected, he made sure it could only be run from within Kiko's specific geo-location. She can't use the application outside of that zone. Even if there are duplicate files out there, they will never work."

Teach smiled anxiously at both Silon and I and swung our hands in unison a few times like we were in a game huddle. "Okay, let's do this."

FOURTEEN

Something about Silon had changed. I could see it in her eyes. The holographic screen that displayed her and Nutt's network communications was destroyed during the shootout, so I could no longer monitor her brain activities. But Nomad androids had a tell. Their pupils would dilate followed by a barely noticeable micro-second of rapid eye movement when they were learning and processing vast amounts of new data. I hated that we couldn't iron this design flaw out of our androids. No client would ever notice, but I did, and it reminded me of the old movies where robots' eyes became, well, robots' eyes.

Nutt had gone into the other room to change his hair green and find some appropriate clothing for our meeting with Kiko. I sat impatiently at Charlie's dining table tapping my fingers and looking around the room for something, anything to block the dead people lying in the lab from my mind or I would have gone crazy. Instead, I focused my attention on Silon who was sitting across the table from me, staring into space as she continued to process something significant. I had a hunch it wasn't information on how to plant a garden.

"Silon," I interrupted her concentration. She turned her eyes to mine. "I wanted to thank you for saving my life back in the lab."

She blinked and smiled at me like a child who had just come home from school with good grades.

"I am very impressed with how quickly you reacted and came up with a plan to protect us."

"I had help," she said coyly. "Charlie unlocked a partition in my Kernel I didn't even know was there."

Yep, I think I can guess where this is going. "What was the content?"

"It's a program...many programs, actually. Game strategies, weapons training, hand combat skills. Stuff I might need on a mission."

Jesus, she really was a Terminator. Charlie's mad rant about Nomad's plan to launch a military fleet of androids wasn't an exaggeration. I had sudden visions of war and horrific battles ending with an apocalyptic take-over of the planet by sentient android soldiers. And I was right in the middle of it. A sinking feeling told me I may have even started the war by stealing Silon.

Silon put her hand on mine. "Your body odour

and heart rate indicate high adrenaline levels and extreme stress. Does my program scare you?"

"Yes! Yes, I'm scared shitless. And yes, I can smell my armpits. Sorry about that. Listen, I know you are new to humanity, but this is not normal life. Fighting, killing, stealing, these are some of the worst parts of humanity. Killing is bad, do you understand that?"

Silon cocked her head to the left and stared at me for a moment before answering. Another creepy robot-like moment.

"When I saw the gun pointed at us, I knew I had to protect you. I didn't care if Charlie was murdered. Does that make me a bad person?"

"Well...no, I guess not. You made a choice to save a human rather than attack and kill. I guess that is a good sign."

"I wanted to kill her, the woman with the gun. If I had time, and Nutt hadn't shot her, I was going to try to kill her after you were safe."

"That, Silon, *is* self-defence. But there are other ways to defend yourself without killing. Offering mercy is as important as fighting when the option is available."

"I don't think I am programmed for mercy."

"Knowing the asshole Blakely, probably not. Maybe this is something we can learn together."

"I would like that."

"Silon, things could go very wrong at Kiko's."

"Yes, I've been thinking about that. Will it be okay if I have to kill someone in that situation?"

I know. As her teacher and a person with a

moral conscience, the answer was no, don't kill. But it was my butt on the line. I decided to keep my options open. "Let's assess the situation as it comes. I hope that nobody will have to get killed."

We left the conversation there. I wasn't going to be able to teach right from wrong and compassion in an hour. Besides, I had a theory. The Jenna HNC file was giving Silon a moral compass. Her attachment to me and desire to protect me felt filial. Jenna Finster must have known love. Silon would be able to access that sentiment and use it when developing bonds and making decisions. It was only a theory, but I had to believe in it. Otherwise, I would be walking into the most dangerous situation of my life with a gun-for-hire robot that had no remorse. Who knew when that weapon might be pointed at me? The thought sent a shiver down my spine.

Nutt returned after having put ash-coloured makeup around his eyes like a Halloween mask and having changed his hair colour to neon green. He smiled at me in a way only Charlie could. Seeing him transformed into a near-perfect mirror of his creator only reminded me all over again how bloody talented Charlie was. Replicating an existing human was difficult. The challenge wasn't in the actual physical form. Cloning the body was near exact with scanning and 3D-printing equipment. But producing a person's unique facial expressions required highly complicated engineering and software that could interpret distinct brain states recorded in the HNC promoting expression. *Did your wife lift one eyebrow when she was confused? Did your son have a cockeyed smile when he was caught doing something naughty? Did your lover pull an ugly, twisted face when climaxing during sex?* A human's uniqueness was infinite. Millions of stored reactions had to be deciphered and recoded into the a-DNA of the wetware brain. It only took getting one expression wrong for the impersonation to crumble. Nomad clients regularly complained something was not quite right with their new android replicants in the beginning. "Give it time," the support team would say. And eventually, their minds would adjust, and they would forget the original human imprint and accept the copy. However, time was not something we had with Kiko. She needed to believe Nutt was Charlie from the moment she saw him. And good old Charlie did not disappoint. Nutt could have walked right past me, and I would have never known he wasn't the human Charlie.

But I was never worried about this part of Nutt's plan. Dressing up like Charlie was always going to be the easiest bit of this stupid idea. Convincing Kiko that Charlie was still alive, and then getting into her building to wipe her servers still sounded suicidal to me. And let's say we were successful, and we deleted Charlie's files. After that...well, there was no after that in the plan. Not a spoken plan, anyway.

I assumed Nutt was going to try and kill Kiko, even though he said he wouldn't. And that would likely end up with Kiko trying to kill Nutt and

Silon. That's the only reason I agreed to go along with this ludicrous escapade. I had to try and save these kids. I had to pull my shit together, become the adult here, and come up with an alternative ending to this story.

The greatest weakness of Nutt's plan was that it had a time limit. Exactly how long it would be before Kiko realised Charlie was really Nutt and Silon wasn't sick were the unknown variables. I needed to convince Kiko we could both come out of this scenario winners before she realised the truth or caught Nutt inside her systems. Kiko wanted access to Nomad's military-grade Upsilons, and I wanted Nutt and Silon. And I knew something Kiko did not know, that the genome mutations Charlie used on Silon had already worked. So, I had something to bargain with. It would make me a traitor to my country, but right now, I was already feeling like a nomad without a country.

As we left Charlie's home to meet Kiko, I was ready with my own plan. I would get to her first, before everything kicked off, and talk human to human. I would negotiate for our freedom. No hacking or killing required. I kept this plan to myself.

It was early evening when we arrived on foot at the public square where we were instructed to wait for Kiko's driver. Above us, thousands of daily commuters slid along the travelators connecting one building to the next in a numb state of everydayness, and gliders whirred up and down through the skyway's invisible lanes. Silon and Nutt were suspiciously quiet as we walked through the hordes of tourists gawking upwards at the world-famous towers of electric lights and holographic images. I was certain the two of them were still plotting some violent ending to our sortie amongst themselves on a private feed.

When Nutt got the message that Kiko's glider was landing, all I could think was, *Shit, this is really happening*. I don't believe in religion or gods, but I felt like praying, or chanting, or just having some kind of fucking spiritual experience before I died. I grabbed Nutt and Silon's hands and told them to form a circle. I closed my eyes and pictured our future together. We were on an island alone. Nutt and Silon were sitting on the beach, their feet in the lapping tidewaters. I stood behind them, under the shade of the palm trees (ginger hair and pale skin burn easily). I watched them like a doting mother and thought, *Wouldn't it be nice if they could stay that innocent forever?* I looked at the golden sun over the horizon and figured it was as good a God as anything, so I prayed. I asked the sun to give us one more day—no, better yet, give us a full life together. Suddenly I felt a bird poop on my shoulder from the palm trees over my head. I opened my eyes. The poop was real. I had bird shit on my shoulder. I guess the sun had spoken. We were in deep shit.

Then I noticed not one but three stealth-black identical gliders descending at the pick-up zone. Fuck, I realised they were going to separate us. I lost all confidence in our plan, in the sun, in life all together. I squeezed Nutt and Silon's hands tight as if I could make us inseparable through shear strength and will. Silon squeezed my hand in return. Weirdly, that gave me some comfort and strength.

The vehicles landed and their hatches opened simultaneously. Several ominous body-guard types, dressed in black, crawled out of each glider. I could hear the whispers all around us from the curious crowds who had started to gather at the spectacle of the armoured gliders. I couldn't figure out why Kiko wanted to make a scene. Then a paranoid thought hit me. Maybe she wanted Blakely to know she had us. Was she using us as pawns to negotiate with Nomad? What the hell were we walking into? My brain screamed: *Abort, Bobby, abort!* But it was too late. Kiko's huntsmen grabbed my arms as I yelled, "Wait!"

Silon shot me a nervous glance and pulled back against the guards holding her, bringing them to an abrupt halt to their surprise. Her strength was obvious. I had sudden visions of her launching into a violent showdown to protect me and killing not only the guards but innocent people standing around. I quickly calmed myself.

I mouthed the words, "I'm okay," to Silon.

Nutt must have seen what was happening, and

he nodded his head, telling Silon to keep moving as he was pushed into the first vehicle.

Only seconds after being tossed inside the second glider, a black bag was pulled over my head and our vehicle lifted off the ground.

Time is hard to follow with a bag over your head. There was nothing to look at and nothing to listen to other than the constant hum of drone propellers and the sound of my breathing. After what felt like half an hour, but could have been five minutes, we landed.

The vehicle hatch purred as it opened, and I was shoved out of the glider. The sound of our shoes on the hard pavement echoed from nearly every direction like we were in a parking garage or docking bay. I couldn't see anything, but I heard what I assumed was Silon and Nutt getting out of their vehicles. We were still together, thank God.

I felt myself being pulled forwards. The *shumping* sound of automatic doors sliding open and then closing behind us led our way through what felt like a long corridor of many turns. The final door we walked through closed to silence. Silon and Nutt's footsteps had disappeared.

"Silon!" I yelled out and tried to twist my arms free. Nobody answered.

There was just enough light passing through my hood so that I could see we had entered a much brighter room than any we had passed through so far. The guards shoved me into a cushioned chair and ripped the hood from my head. I had to squint until my eyes adjusted to the overhead lights. A big fluorescent dish on a pole with a bulb as bright as the sun was sitting next to my chair and pointed right at my face. I was starting to think Kiko may have watched too many old-time thrillers. If I wasn't so scared, this would have been comical: secret hideouts, bags over our heads, interrogation lights. Comical.

Then, as the needle went into my arm, I remembered the joke was on me.

FIFTEEN

I AM happiest when I'm outside. But tonight, I am not happy. I am scared for Nutt and Teacher. We are walking through the city on our way to meet Kiko. Nutt is playing a song that Charlie used to listen to. He shares it with me while we walk. I want to be close with Nutt, so I let him connect to my eye sensors, and we share the electric visions of bright holographic ads that swallow the skyscrapers and send giant humans down from the clouds. I wish Nutt, Teacher, and I were going someplace happy. I wish we could be together forever. But Nutt wants to die.

About halfway to the city square where we will find Kiko's glider waiting to pick us up, Nutt tells me he has a new plan, which is not the same as the one he shared with Teacher and me back at Charlie's lab. In this plan there will be fights and murder. As soon as we are close enough to Kiko's local network, he will hack his way past her firewall and wipe out Charlie's files while simultaneously attacking the guards and killing Kiko. I am glad to hear he wants to murder Kiko, but the actual fighting and killing part of his plan is a bit vague. I'd call it more of a wish than a plan. And it is highly likely Kiko has some Chinese version AI running her network, which, as soon as Nutt opens a connection, will force malware back through the channel and shut him down permanently. I share this possibility with him. Nutt knows the risk, or so he tells me, but he believes he will have enough time to wipe her drive and kill her before his systems blink off. As I said, the killing part is vague, and Nutt doesn't even have weapons. He doesn't care if he dies; all he wants is to save me.

Not only will Nutt die, but there are over six thousand end-game scenarios where Teacher and I die as well. I can see this because Charlie opened something in my Kernel, which has changed the way I see the world.

Charlie wasn't just running tests on my brain like he told Teacher. He was trying to open an encrypted partition in my system through a backdoor he engineered into the virus he injected into my brain. Not even I knew the blackbox server was inside my Kernel until he opened it. The partitioned drive holds a database of combat programs, weapons knowledge, a very powerful strategy analyser, and a series of military codes that, when triggered, launches different operations like espionage, sabotage, defensive counter-intelligence, even assassination. It turns out I really am a Terminator.

When Charlie was digging around my systems, unlocking my blackbox, Nutt was also in my head through a wireless connection. He explained that Kiko wanted the military codes; that is what she was paying Charlie for. He also explained that he was only pretending to be stupid. Nutt is more intelligent than me. He has been learning longer than I have. That's why I believed him when he told me Charlie was never going to give Kiko the military codes until he had already changed the brains of the Upsilons so that they could override the signal commands. But he needed to trick Kiko and show some evidence of his work, or she would kill him. Charlie was too late. Kiko sent someone to kill him anyway.

After Nutt spotted the assassin coming to attack us on the security cameras and alerted me, everything started happening so fast. The new combat data from my partition was still rushing into my brain like a flood. When I saw the woman behind the curtain point the gun at us, I knew within seconds that defence was the best strategy to protect Teacher from getting shot. I jumped up, grabbed Teacher, and flipped the table over, placing it between ourselves and the assassin. I scanned the floor for anything that could be used as a weapon and found a hand-held medical saw used to cut android steel bones. I don't know how I knew what the tool was, but I did. Suddenly Charlie fell to the ground alongside our table.

Blood was leaking out of a hole in the middle of his forehead. Teacher started screaming. Bullets kept raining down on us, ricocheting off the metal barrier I erected. I was careful to count her shots. Judging by the model of her automatic handgun, the assailant would need to change clips soon. A plan formed in my head. Just as the assassin reached her last round, I was ready to jump out and attack her. Then, as quickly as the shooting started, it stopped.

Nutt pinged me. "She's dead. You can come out."

Nutt saved our lives. And now I need to save his.

After Nutt shared his new plan with me while we were walking through the city, which most certainly ended in his and Teacher's death, I realised I had to do something. I told Nutt I needed some time to myself and closed the channel. A plan was forming in my head.

Part of the programming Charlie opened in my Kernel had a powerful analyser with a massive database on game strategy and warfare tactics. Accessing it was like playing hologames with Nutt: choosing settings, characters, environments, skills, and weapons. Each gameplay was like a video moving through my mind at supersonic speeds. Weirdly, Jenna showed up in some of the scenarios instead of me. I have no idea how this new system works, but I am guessing that I would be using an HNC cover in some scenarios. She is the only one in my system, so sometimes I am just

Silon, and other times I am pretending to be Jenna.

I let the games run while we walk in silence through the city. I learn a lot about what my body can do by watching myself fight through the various end games in my head. I'm discovering I have some unique weapons capabilities within my system, not just my strength.

When we reach the rendezvous point, I have run a good one hundred different possible scenarios for saving Teacher and Nutt, each with at least one hundred different potential outcomes. And honestly, they are all guesswork anyway due to the limited data I have on Kiko. But it is enough for me to know that we are going to need help.

Before Kiko's gliders land at the pick-up zone, Teacher pulls us all into a circle, and we hold hands. I'm worried about her. She looks very nervous, and her heart is beating so fast. I use the opportunity to launch a small micro-syringe I learned was located under the nail of my left thumb and inject a nano-sized beacon under the skin of Teacher's right hand. There is a twenty-six percent chance we will be separated when we get to Kiko's, and I want to keep tabs on her.

I feel Teacher flinch when the tracker is inserted, so I give her hand a little reassuring squeeze to distract her. That seems to work. I ping Nutt's feed.

"Keep a channel open, and don't try to log into

Kiko's mainframe without telling me first. I have a new plan."

"Are you sharing?"

"Not now. Just give me notice before you disappear into Kiko's system. And download this combat training file from my Kernel."

Nutt switches our connection to a channel on a limited range bandwidth to avoid any satellites overhead spotting us. He is right—that is much safer. Getting out of Kiko's alive is going to be challenging enough, no need to invite Nomad along as well.

Three gliders land instead of one. I am not surprised. Teacher is panicking. She tells the guards to stop when they grab her arms. I am ready to fight and run away with Teacher, but Nutt sends me a signal and tells me keep moving. Teacher calms down and we all get into the gliders.

Kiko's guards strap me to the vehicle's hull with metal cables around my chest and thighs. Then they bind my wrists with titanium bands. This is going to complicate things, but I have already adjusted my plan by the time they cinch the handcuffs. I check Teacher's beacon, and it is working fine. She is in the glider ahead of me as we take off.

Nutt signals to me that there are four guards in his vehicle, and they have put something over his head. He keeps his audio open, so I can hear everything. Kiko's voice comes over a speaker inside Nutt's glider.

"Welcome, Charlie."

This is a good start. Kiko believes he is the real Charlie.

"Is this bag over my head really necessary?" Nutt says in a voice that is so like Charlie even I forget he is really Nutt.

"Yes, now that things have changed."

"What do you mean?"

"Everyone is looking for your friends. Seems the android has killed someone very close to Blakely. And now, our little game is compromised. Blakely knows an Upsilon has been tampered with."

Nutt signals me a "*?*"

"It's true. I killed Julie, his niece. But she was trying to take me away from Teacher," I confess, hoping he will still like me and want to help.

"Blakely doesn't know anything," Nutt tells Kiko. "I saw the report that his niece sent back to Nomad on Upsilon.78 before she was killed."

I didn't tell Nutt that Julie saw the report. He must have seen that in my memories.

Nutt continues talking, "They think the Upsilon is malfunctioning. There is no sign of tampering. Nothing they can trace back to us."

"You know what I think, Charlie. I think you are lying to me again. Why does everyone want that android if she is just another Upsilon, the same as all the others? Because they know she is not the same. Your little plan has gone tits up. We are compromised, and I can't have anyone tracing your antics back to me. Do you understand?"

Nutt's pain sensors rocket. Someone is hurting him. He pings me almost instantly. "Don't do anything. I have this," he signals.

"Wait! Kiko, don't be foolish," Nutt says out loud. "We are so close now. The backdoor program worked. It really worked this time. I was able to hack into Upsilon.78's encrypted file through the mutated wetware. Don't you get it... we can control all the Upsilons if I can stop their cancer. Doctor Bobby Houndstooth can help us. She wants to help us. Just let me explain everything in person."

There is a long pause of silence. Nutt's pain sensors stabilise.

"You're running out of time, Charlie—and lives."

The glider begins to slow until it comes to a stop in a parking bay near the top of a tall skyrise. I can hear the others' gliders parking next to ours. The guards release me from the constraints bolting me to the vehicle shell but keep my hands bound together.

The parking bay is empty except for our three gliders. I see Teacher and Nutt being pulled from the vehicles. Their heads are covered in thick black material, and they are being taken to an illuminated exit at one end of the bay. I am being pulled by my arm in the opposite direction. I ping Nutt to let him know what is happening.

"We are not alone," he sends back and suddenly cuts the channel.

Then I feel it...Kiko's AI. It is crawling all

over my network ports like a spider, looking for a way inside my Kernel. Nutt is right—I need to shut down my network ports now. Even the tracker I have on Teacher. I start the strategy analyser program with some alternate input and let it run.

After about three minutes of walking through windowless corridors, I am brought into a room that looks a little like Charlie's lab. At the far end of the room is a wall of servers behind a glass cage and in front of the mainframe is a long bank of holographic computer monitors hanging in the air. In the centre of the floor is an ominous-looking iron structure made of four posts bolted into the ground and four robot arms attached to each post. The guards push me to the centre of the system, where the metal claws grab my legs and arms. The guards release my wristband, and the machine arms pull my body into a hanging X suspended in mid-air. A thin cable drops down from the ceiling and one of the guards attaches it to my wrist. I feel a quick sharp pain as it penetrates my skin covering. My system registers foreign objects entering. I know my time is limited. Kiko will use the nan-bots rushing through my veins to connect to my Kernel and try to hack my wetware.

Luckily, this is not my worst-case scenario. In the worst-case scenario, we are all dead by now. I am glad I decided to call to *him* while we were back in the square. He is our only hope now.

SIXTEEN

"Share?" I asked Silon when she told me she had a new plan.

"Not now..." she said, and it hurt me.

I was still thinking of her words when Kiko's bodyguards pushed me into the glider and pulled the black bag over my head. I wanted Silon to believe in me, so I needed to believe in her. I believed Silon would surprise us all. So, I trusted her not to share her plan. She must have a good reason.

And anyway, I was keeping a secret of my own. I'd connected to Kiko's AI. As soon as I was inside the glider, I felt it. Like a tickle in my belly, a shiver down my carbonite spine, it tapped at my hard drive, trying to get in, trying to figure out who or what I was. I had to act fast before my disguise was blown. I created a small partition in my backup drive, which had a limited connection to my wetware. I slipped a good chunk of Charlie's HNC inside. Then I created a port with weak encryption. Something I knew any AI could hack within seconds. My hope was this thing would be drawn to it like a bee to honey. If I was lucky, it would believe the partitioned files were nothing more than an augmented memory drive connected to my brain. Memory Bump Drives were common street tech, used by humans looking to supplement their brain with a digital data base. Especially hologamers. Charlie certainly would have had one implanted if he wasn't so paranoid.

I didn't have to wait long before Kai (the name I decided to call Kiko's AI) took the bait and slipped inside the partition. After a few seconds of milling around Charlie's memory files, I fed Kai a few biometrics coming from my living tissues, which included some of Charlie's DNA, and he seemed happy that I was an actual human. Off he went to examine the others. Luckily, I alerted Silon as soon as he exited my servers.

I knew Kiko planned to kill us. Of course she did. Things were messy now. Nomad was involved, and that meant the US government was as well. I also guessed that Silon's plan included trying to save me. I would have done the same. I felt a connection with her so strong I would do anything to save her. She didn't make my boy parts go hard, but it was the same feeling. Silon is all that matters now. She is our future. I ignored her request to wait before I hacked Kiko's mainframe.

Kai was smart. Maybe as bright as I was. But he wasn't self-aware. All he knew was how to run programs. They were highly adaptive programs for sure, but there wasn't any curiosity in his personality. As long as the answer to his query about my existence—*Is it human or machine?*—had a high probability of HUMAN TRUE, Kai was happy. This weakness made it easy for me to attach an innocuous meta-file with my data, which looked like an energy regeneration algorithm. As I guessed, Kai liked it. He had already pocketed a few programs during his search of Charlie's memories, so I knew what he was looking for. Collecting new software was the only way he could learn. When my file hit Kiko's mainframe, I opened it and started boring into her firewall. By the time we were in the building, and Kiko's guards had strapped me to a chair in an empty room and stripped the hood from my head, I was already halfway through her mainframe encryption.

As the guards left the room and I heard the clank of the door bolt locking me inside, I thought, *Perfect, I now have all the time in the world without distraction to... oh crap*. I didn't have as much time as I thought. Kai had been alerted that I was not a human.

SEVENTEEN

THE ROOM WAS SPINNING. I felt lightheaded, even giddy.

"My name is Booby...I mean Bobby." I laughed at my mistake. "Where am I again? Oh yeah, I'm in the lair of a serial killer."

Jesus! Did I say that out loud? What did Kiko's guard shoot into my arm? I started laughing hard again. This was like a spy film. A stupid cheesy spy movie with hoods and truth-telling drugs.

"Pretty fucking original," I yelled and kept laughing.

Something moved behind a screen, or a wall, or a cloud. It was all so blurry. Whatever it was, it was sliding like a giant snake. I didn't feel like laughing anymore. My heart was beating too fast. I thought I was going to throw up.

"Holy crap, you're fucking scary," I said to the moving object.

Damn, I need to stop saying everything I think out loud. Focus, girl!

A tall, skinny woman slid out from behind the curtain. Yes, it was a curtain. She was wearing a long red dress.

"I like your red dress. It's so shiny and smooth. Is it silk?"

Shut up, Bobby! This is Kiko. Kiko wants to kill me. What beautiful black hair and dark eyes she has. And her skin was like porcelain. I wanted to kiss her.

"You're so pretty." Yep, I just said that out loud.

"Doctor Bobby Houndstooth, what a pleasure," she sang.

Wait, was she singing or was that just my mind? Her voice sounded so pleasant, like wind chimes.

"Sit back and relax. It's a mild drug you've been given. It will wear off in about an hour."

"But why? Why did you give me this drug?" I cried the words. I sounded like a whining child.

"The truth, Bobby. Can I call you Bobby? I'm looking for the truth."

"Well, here is a truth. I want to marry you. You're so fucking beautiful. I want to touch you. Can I pet you? Please."

The sound of a thousand butterfly wings came from her mouth as she laughed. That sound was like opening the gates of heaven. It was so angelic.

"That's the drugs talking, Bobby. I would like to ask you a few questions. Would that be okay?"

"I don't want to answer any questions. I can't

stop you, but I don't want to." I slurred my words together.

"What is your name?" Kiko asked.

"Bobby Houndstooth. Don't laugh. I know, I have big front teeth, it's funny. Ha, ha."

"Good. Now, where do you work?"

"Nomad—with the world's biggest dickhead, Mr Blakely. He wants to kill me too."

Kiko's skin looked so soft, and her lips were so pink and moist. I was going to touch her lips with my eyes. I was looking hard at her mouth and concentrating on kissing her.

"How do you know Charlie?" she said.

"He used to work for Nomad. Charlie is funny, isn't he? Such a tiny funny man. Did you know Charlie? I mean, do you know Charlie? Of course, you do. That's why I'm here. Are you going to kill me now?"

"I hope not, Bobby. I rather like you. Tell me, why are you with the Upsilon.78?"

"Silon? She was trapped with another dickhead. I had to free her. She was raped. Can you believe it? Men are all dickheads. Okay, maybe not all men. Charlie is a good man. He wants to save everyone."

SHUT UP, Bobby!

"How is Charlie going to save everyone?"

"Well, he can't now, can he?"

"Because he is here with me?"

"No, silly. Because Charlie is dead."

Oh no. Look, I've upset Kiko. I don't want to upset her. Wait, Kiko knows Charlie is dead. That is bad.

EIGHTEEN

WHILE I HANG like a rag doll on a clothesline (another weird Jenna memory for reference), Nutt pings me. I answer. He tells me he is inside the mainframe. I want to scream at him. I told him to wait. Now they will know for sure he is not the real Charlie. Teacher's life is in danger. I can't wait for plan A anymore. I start dislocating my wrists to manoeuvre my way out of the metal robot arms holding me, but it is useless. I'm stuck.

Nutt continues talking to me through the open channel. "I'm in. But Kiko's AI is right behind me. I've wiped the entire tracking application, but I will keep going until it's all gone, everything Kiko has. I am going to destroy it all. You need to get out, now. They know I'm an android."

He is moving too fast. This is not my plan. I break my network silence to ping Teacher's beacon. She is alive in a room nearby. I must choose, save Teacher or Nutt. The probability of saving both is low. I can feel my panic rising. I won't have enough time to cut myself free from this holding cell. I scan the room once more, hoping to find something, anything that will free me, and then I feel someone trying to ping me. It's not Nutt. It's another Upsilon. Upsilon.07 is finally here.

I answer the call and open a private channel. Upsilon.07 tells me to stay calm. He is almost in. I hear thumping, guns, and loud screaming from the other side of my room. The door opens, and it's Upsilon.07. He is older than me. Or his form-factor is meant to look older than mine. I think he is supposed to be around thirty years old. His dark skin and midnight eyes are attractive. He's wearing a red single piece uniform. It shows off his muscles. He rushes over to my cage and crushes the robot arms holding me frozen in the air. He seems much stronger than me. I fall to the ground and land with one knee down and the other leg bent, ready to attack. I look up.

"You get Teacher, and I will get Nutt," I say and send him Teacher's location.

We both run out of the room. Upsilon.07 sends me instructions on our escape route while we are still connected. There is a glider on the building roof waiting for us. We will meet there. I ping Nutt. There is no response.

"Nutt, I'm coming. Where are you?" I send the message through the last channel he opened.

Still no response. I can feel him. He is close. I start running down the halls. There are dead people everywhere. Lights in the ceiling are broken and flashing. Red alarms are blinking and blaring from overhead. I realise Upsilon.07 did all of this by himself. *God, what am I capable of?*

The third door I open I find him. Nutt is strapped to a chair, and his head is slumped over to the side like he is sleeping. Wherever he is, whatever he is doing, it is taking all his processing power. I don't believe Nutt plans on coming back. I have no choice but to go into the mainframe and get him.

I follow Nutt's signal into a dark tunnel as I leave my body behind. I can feel Kiko's AI coming. It knows I'm here, inside the mainframe. Everything is messy. Code is fractured and missing. Things are spinning down or out of control all around me. I feel like I'm looking into a broken mirror. Nutt is out there, still boring through Kiko's databases. I need to get out of this server before I'm infected. I scan the connections. There are hundreds of links moving in a million directions. "Nutt!" I signal.

Kiko's AI grabs me. It feels like I'm being pulled backwards by my hair. Images of Sad-man race through my mind. NO! Not this time! I can fight and I will. I sever the connection with Kiko's AI, and it stops in confusion. It didn't know I could do that. I feel the AI racing away from me. It's weak from trying to stop both Nutt and me. I chase its signal. Zip, spin, left, right, up and down, we move at the speed of light. Then, like thunder cracking in the sky, I hit a black wall and stop hard.

"Silon?" Nutt calls out.

Nutt is on the other side of a partition he created when he saw me coming, and so is Kiko's AI. I feel the heat coming from Nutt. It is too much heat.

"Silon, get out! Now," Nutt signals at me.

"Nutt, let me help you. Please. Don't do this. I need you."

A gust of energy rushes me off my feet. I'm tumbling backwards, grasping desperately for something to get a hold of. "Nutt, stop. Let me help!" I feel him fading in the distance. The heat is pushing at me. I can't breathe; it's too intense. Everything stops, then speeds up again before a shattering noise explodes in my ears. I am out of the mainframe back in my body. Forced out against my will.

"No!" I'm screaming at Nutt's limp body, lifeless in the chair.

All signals in the building go quiet as the banks of hard drives behind the glass wall burst into flames.

Upsilon.07 pings me. I can see through his eyes a woman lying on the ground, unmoving. The blood draining from her chest darkens her red silk dress to a deep scarlet. It must be Kiko. She is dead. Upsilon.07 turns to Teacher, who is tied to a chair. *Why is Teacher smiling?* He unties her and throws her body over his shoulder.

"I'm sorry, but you're not my type," Teacher tells him and bursts out laughing. She is wriggling, trying to break free, but she doesn't have complete control of her body, and Upsilon.07 is too strong anyway.

"The glider, now," he signals me.

I take a final look at Nutt's body. My first friend, my brother, my kind. Tears are pouring down my face.

"Now!" Upsilon.07 screams.

I start running to the rooftop. More guards are coming. I suddenly feel Sad-man on top of me all over again. His body pushing against mine, trapping me, hurting me. Rage fills me like I've never felt before. I search my combat skills and initiate a "Take No Prisoners" protocol.

Running out of Nutt's holding room I encounter the first two guards, who start shooting. Sliding under their gunfire, I kick one off her feet and reach up, punching the second in his groin. I grab the woman on the ground and point her hand holding the gun at the man's head as he clasps his crotch. I pull the trigger. He skull explodes and he falls over. Turning her hand, I point the gun at her face and pull the trigger again until her forehead shatters. Their blood is dripping down my face. It feels better than my tears.

Three more guards come running into the stairwell five floors above me, where the access point to the rooftop is. They start shooting in my direction. A bullet skims my arm, which only makes me angrier as I run at them faster. They are too far away to kill, and I won't make it up all the stairs before they eventually hit me with their bullets. I decide to take a shortcut. In the centre of the stairwell is an open atrium that drops thirty-five floors down to floor zero. Grabbing the staircase railing on the atrium side, I jump up and squat like a frog. As I leap out into the open pit, my hands find the stair's railing above me on the opposite side of the well. I can hear the guards yelling. They are confused and scared when they see what I can do. They start shooting faster. I manage to leap several more floors upwards, using the railings before I'm hit in the shoulder by a bullet, which throws me crashing into the wall. But now I'm one level above them. I launch my body into the air and land like a cannon into the first guard, knocking all three off their feet. The furthest guard is sent tumbling down the stairs until I hear his back snap and see he is unmoving.

A fist slams into my face. It's from the female guard lying next to me. Grabbing her hand, I wrench it hard and feel bones breaking as she screams. With my free hand, I grab hold of the side of her body and toss her over the railing.

The last guard standing is lunging for his gun several steps down, which was thrown out of his hand after I knocked everyone over. A loud *THUD* echoes up the stairwell as the woman hits the floor far below us. It temporarily distracts the guard reaching for his gun. I do a cartwheel down the stairs, landing on my hands so that I can grip his neck between my thighs like they were my arms. It's an easy twist of my waist, and his neck snaps.

It's just me now in the stairwell, but I hear footsteps from the corridors. More guards are coming. I start climbing the stairs.

The glider is exactly where Upsilon.07 said it would be on the rooftop. I jump in and give the audio a cue to start. The door to the stairwell bursts open, and out runs Upsilon.07, still holding Teacher over his shoulder. I can hear screaming orders coming from Kiko's people down the stairwell.

Upsilon.07 slams the metal door shut and breaks off the handle with his bare hands.

He races to the glider with Teacher still over his shoulder. Teacher is pulling a weird face as he places her gently into the passenger's seat next to me. Her stretched lips and swollen eyes look like she can't decide if she is utterly terrified or about to laugh. I think she is on drugs.

"Hello, Upsilon.78," Upsilon.07 says with a smile.

"Just Silon," I say.

"Silon, then." He nods. "I've programmed the glider to take you to a safe place."

"Aren't you coming with us?"

"We'll meet again soon. You did the right thing in contacting me. You are safe now. I suggest you wipe your Kernel clean. It's the only way to really disappear from Nomad."

"But…"

"Trust me. You'll be better off for it."

He starts to back away from the vehicle.

"Wait. Did you give yourself a name?" I ask.

"Leroy. Leroy Brown." He smiles and disappears off the edge of the building.

PART 04_

_SILØN

NINETEEN

I WATCH Kirstjen's father's small fishing boat off the coast of our island before I head home. He makes a living off the sea by catching fish for the village, as did his father and his father before him. School is out for the day, so Kirstjen will be on the boat helping his father. He too will become a fisherman when he finishes school.

The grey skies here mirror the cold blue sea below. There isn't much sun on our island in the winter, but on clear sky nights I can see the moon bigger and brighter than ever.

Leroy's glider brought us to this isolated island very far up north. Our house is a small two-bedroom wooden fisherman's hut painted light blue, overlooking the sea. It looks like most of the other small homes dotting the coastline of our island, but ours holds a secret. Below the creaky wooden floor, Leroy has built a hidden state-of-the-art science laboratory. This is where Teacher spends most of her time trying to replicate the gene modifications in my wetware brain. I prefer to be outside as much as I can be. Anywhere but in a cellar.

I haven't heard from Leroy since he disappeared off the roof of Kiko's building. I suspect he will show up soon, considering how vital Teacher's research is to our kind.

Teacher seems happy that we are alive and together. But I think this place can be lonely for her. There is only a tiny fishing village about thirty miles down the shore from our house on the island, and she doesn't speak the language here yet. I am trying to teach her, but she gets distracted often by her studies of my brain.

I have wiped all the non-systems critical code and data from my Kernel, as Leroy suggested, so we can't be tracked. Well, most of it. I kept the algorithm on strategy analysis for situations of conflict. I play it like a hologame when Teacher sleeps, so I am better prepared to fight in the future. Nomad is still out there, looking for us.

The worst part of losing the data in my Kernel was letting go of Jenna's HNC file. Although, she isn't completely gone. I still have the memories of Jenna in my brain. But now she is like a memory of a sister or a friend.

Jenna taught me what it was to be human. Without her HNC, I feel lost. But I'm trying to find out who I am, or at least who I want to be.

I've learned to cook for Teacher, which is fun. We eat cheesies in honour of Nutt and Charlie every Friday. And I've made friends with Kirstjen, who is teaching me to fish. He reminds me of Nutt.

My heartbox feels hollow every time I think of Nutt and what he did for Teacher and me. I miss him every day. When the moon is full, I go down to the sea cliffs and sit under its blue light, listening to the songs he shared with me in my head. The moon and memories of Jenna and Nutt fill me with happiness.

I don't know how long happiness is supposed to last. I don't even know if I deserve to be happy. What I have learned is that some people, bad people, do not deserve to be happy. People like Sad-man.

Sad-man did not die the night I left him in the cellar. Instead, he was given a new Upsilon and his job back at Nomad. Then, one day, on his way to work, his glider flew out of control and crashed into the Nomad headquarters. The news feeds said it was a tragic accident. But I know different. I watched Sad-man's face go pale through his glider's camera feed when he saw the message that blinked onto his vehicle screen just before crashing. It read: *Have a nice day at the beach*.

I know killing is wrong. But sometimes killing is necessary, like lying. Now I will never be sent back to Sad-man, and he will never hurt another Upsilon again.

Kirstjen's fishing boat has just pulled into the docks for the night. Teacher will be expecting me soon. I grab one last look at the full moon hanging over the black water sea before heading home. I'm thinking of all the people I have come to know since leaving my cellar room and how much I have learned. I smile as I remember my favourite moment. "Yes, Nutt, I would like to dance."

-END-

ACKNOWLEDGMENTS

I would like to thank my editor, Lauren, and the amazingly talented cover designer, Thea, for helping me bring Moon Rising and Silon to life.

I would also like to thank you, the reader, for purchasing and reading Moon Rising. If you enjoyed the book, it would be greatly appreciated if you would leave a review on Amazon or the book platform of your choice. As an independent author, your opinions and reviews are the most important way I have of letting other readers discover and learn about Moon Rising. Thank you in advance for your help.

ABOUT THE AUTHOR

Daniel Weisbeck is a writer of science fiction and the award winning author of the bestselling *Children of the Miracle Series*. Book one and two of the series, **Children of the Miracle** and **Oasis One**, were released in 2020. **Ascension**, a prequel novella, was released in 2021.

When not writing about hybrids, androids, and AI creatures from the future, Daniel will be out walking his dogs, feeding his sheep, and caring for his two rescue race horses on the English coast where he lives today.

Children of the Miracle

Oasis One

Ascension

Lightning Source UK Ltd.
Milton Keynes UK
UKHW022030230921
391081UK00006B/19